TERRAN CUMMANDO
A Novel Of The Sensual Suns

by Frank Sol

Chapter One

"Angelino, Lou?"

"That's me." I straightened to full attention and then snapped off a crisp salute. Then I just stood there and stared intently at my commanding officer as he paced across the deck towards me.

Major Collin Duncan was a short, wiry individual. He had a well-trimmed reddish beard on his face and an assortment of ribbons on his chest. "Welcome to the *Vindication*." He wore the standard grey uniform of the Terran Colonial Guard and made the cotton cloth look like a suit of battle armour.

"Thank you, Major." I was also wearing a standard grey uniform and my kit bag was still on my back. The shuttle bay was behind me and blue-uniformed technicians were moving around the shuttle, servicing it, and taking no notice of either of us.

"I assume that you can find your way around?"

I nodded. "Yes, Sir." *I found my way here from the shuttle bay, didn't I? One frigate is just like any other,* I thought. *The military favours standardized designs for just about everything after all. Anything to cut costs and save money. Right down to the drab paint and subdued lighting.* "I should be able to find my way around the ship."

"We have a schedule and a set shipboard routine here. I suggest you memorize it. Quickly."

"Yes, Sir."

Collin frowned at me. "You've just transferred here from duty dirt-side. I don't care where you came from or what officers you used to serve under. I have one simple rule for you to understand: I am one step below God to you."

I kept my face expressionless, listening to the soft hum of the ventilation system. *Same old speech from every CO I serve with. Nothing in the Guard ever changes.*

"This frigate is one of the forefront vessels in subduing the rebellion," Collin continued. "We colonial marines are the first to be thrown into battle when the fighting gets close and personal."

"I know that, Sir."

"Then you likely also know that we took fairly heavy losses in the last campaign. You are part of the replacements we are being issued. Try to remember that Twenty-First Regiment has a long and honourable history to live up too. We take our name seriously."

The Truculent Lancers *were a storied unit.* "That history is part of the reason I requested assignment to this particular ship, Sir."

"Right now, you are *fresh meat*." Collin smiled rather nastily at me. "The squad likes fresh meat."

I said nothing.

After a long moment, Collin finally nodded. "Dismissed."

* * *

I stepped into the barracks and frowned. Two bunks. *Only two?* I was used to sharing with a dozen or more guys. The cabin was fairly small, so at least having the beds stacked would give us the illusion of space. *The perils of life aboard ship, I guess.*

I tossed my kit bag into one of the storage lockers built into the footboard of the bunks. "Welcome to life in the Terran Marines," I told myself.

I was proud to be here. I was one of seven hundred men and women in the Battalion, supported by one hundred and eight combat vehicles, assigned to defending the ideals of the multi-planetary federation. Or enforcing the whims of the Terran Government which was probably more likely.

"It all sounded so much glorious in the recruiting vids," I said aloud. "So far, there has been a distinct lack of glory."

My erstwhile bunk-mate was gone. "On duty or leave?" I wondered. The *Vindication* was holding station in orbit above

Consecon. The room was devoid of personal touches, giving me no hints as to the character or personality of my room-mate.

"Brad Grazley." That was all I knew about him. And I only knew that much because he'd left some papers on the desk. I didn't want to snoop, but if he was leaving things out in the open for anyone to stumble across...a letter home wasn't all that exciting.

I changed into a tee-shirt and shorts. "An hour or two working out should help me settle in." I headed for the gym.

* * *

"You lost already?"

I stepped through the door into the gym. A few of the other marines present looked up as the hatch hissed closed.

"Look at this one," someone called out.

"Look at that haircut."

"Bout time we got some fresh meat."

I nodded to them, but said nothing. *I am the new guy.* I knew that I would have to prove myself before they would accept me. *Same ritual everywhere...but it's been a while since I was the newbie.*

I hefted weights for a good hour or so. Most of the other guys ignored me.

Sweaty and tired, I headed into the showers. I stripped off my tee-shirt and shorts and cranked the hot water.

"Raw meat on the hoof."

I caught sight of my face in one of the mirrors. I had green eyes set high on a face with strong Greek features. My dark hair was cut short in the current marine style. I liked what I saw, and so did a lot of other guys. I finished showering, only half-listening to the bantering of the other guys in the showers.

"Look at the rug on him."

"We should take the wire cutters to it."

"My mother could use a new coat for the winter."

I shook my head. "You're just jealous," I told my squad-mates as they finished up their own showers. "Your mothers probably have more hair on their chests than you."

Laughter and backslapping signalled my temporary victory in the war of words. All part of the camaraderie of the Guard.

The banter continued in the mess hall.

"Do you all smell that!"

I stood in line, trying to ignore the gesturing marine.

"Looks like we got us a new fish." He sauntered towards me, a cocky swagger in his movements. "What's your name, fish?"

"Lou Angelino." I looked him over. "And you are?"

"Fred Van Der Hagen."

"We call him *Freddie.*"

Fred turned and glared at the other marine. "Fuck off, Mikael."

The red-headed marine grinned back at him. "Only if you promise to keep your hands off me while you watch."

Fred's face darkened.

The line moved forward.

Fred turned back towards me. Fred was shorter than me, but a scar down his right cheek hinted at previous action. His muscular arms strained the brown sleeves of his tee-shirt. "Listen up, Fish. You're on the *Vindication* now, one of the best ships in the whole fucking Fleet. You won't let us down."

"Is that a threat?"

"Just a promise." He clenched his hands into tight fists. "No one slacks off here."

I stood my ground.

"You just might do," he said at last. "At least you look like a soldier and not like the school boys we've been getting from this dirt ball." He turned and strutted away to join a table full of his pals.

Nice ass in those pants. I took my tray and sat down at a table.

* * *

A real hunk of a man walked into the barracks that night. "Hi, I'm Brad."

"Lou." I gave him a look. He was a pretty typical jarhead, about six feet tall, with short sandy blond hair, brown eyes, and perfect teeth. He seemed real nice, but that was just my first impression. I found out very quickly that he had a way of being welcoming and comfortable, but intimidating as well.

"The newbie. I heard that you'd transferred in."

"Word travels fast."

"Yep, it usually does." He shrugged. "I was on a training session." Sweat was soaking his brown tee-shirt and I'll never forget that first view as he undressed to take a shower. He wasn't bashful as he stripped off and covered himself with a white towel—but life in the military quickly stripped away any modesty we might have had to start with. I found myself admiring his smooth chest and well-defined six-pack.

When he returned to our room, I found myself wanting to catch a better look, and everything under the towel was as beautiful as the rest.

Our first night in the room went very smoothly. The bunk beds were old—probably as old as the frigate—and creaked as he got into bed. Brad slept in the nude, and watching him jump into bed was very interesting. From the very first night, we found ourselves talking for hours about every possible thing.

Our friendship grew during the first weeks. Brad had been the last new guy into the squad, so we tended to stick together. One night, about two weeks after transferring in, I awoke in the middle of the night, an unusual occurrence for me. It took me a few seconds to realize what had aroused me. At first it was a slight movement, and I realized that Brad was shaking the bunks. I was then fully aware that he was jerking off!

I lay quietly and listened to the slight movements and his breathing. When his breath caught in his throat, I knew that he had just cum, and I was even more aroused. *What did his cock look like?* I wondered.

Brad rolled over and I listened as his breathing indicated he was asleep. My own arousal needed to be dealt with, and I slipped my boxer shorts down below my balls, and very carefully began to rub and stroke myself to orgasm. It was difficult to be quiet, but I managed to keep my groans down as I shot all over my tummy. It was more powerful than usual, which confused me.

Over the next few weeks, I was periodically aware of Brad jerking off. I never said or did anything, but always repeated his release with one of my own.

Chapter Two

A few weeks after I arrived, we shipped out for a training session dirt-side. Consecon was Brad's homeworld, so he had taken some leave time to visit his family. I had a week of private quarters in our garrison post. It was boring as hell so I was really glad when Brad came back near lights off one night, though he looked pretty down.

"I thought you just had leave," I said.

"I did."

"So why the long face? I thought you were all excited to go off and see your girlfriend."

"I was," he replied. "Cynthia is a great women, and I love her. You know we're getting married in a year or so."

"Yeah, you've mentioned it once or twice."

"She wants to be celibate till then. Man, this is going to kill me, and I don't have a choice."

"That's a tough one, buddy. I bet it will be hard," I said with all sincerity.

"Is that some fucking joke? It's not very funny," Brad said.

I blushed. "Sorry, I didn't mean that as a joke." I couldn't help smile as I got the irony.

Brad also smirked, and we both started laughing. I had some beers hidden in my locker and hastily cracked two of them open. We talked for hours that night, and touched some pretty personal topics.

After we were in bed, unable to see each other, the subject of sex came up again.

"I guess I'll be jerking off just like you from now on," Brad announced.

"What do you mean 'just like me'?" I asked.

"Well, I just figured that's what you did, and...you've woken me up a few

times."

"Well, Mr. Hot Shot, you've woken me up a few times yourself." I could feel my face flush with embarrassment, and I felt myself begin to get an erection. "I guess we both know that we jerk off."

There was a moment of brief silence.

"How much do you...you know...jerk off?"

Growing ever more aroused by the sexual conversation, I didn't hesitate to reply. "Almost every day, sometimes twice."

"I thought I was pretty weird, but even when Cynthia and I were...you know...I still needed to jerk off a couple times per week."

"Yeah, I noticed. This bunk bed tells all." I was already playing with myself as we talked. *So, now it should be my turn to ask a personal question.* "So what's your favourite way to...uh...beat off?"

"I used to use magazines a lot, when I had my own room. With you down below, I just try to remember a hot time...and...just stroke."

My hand was getting a little more active. "I like hand lotion, getting it real slippery." I was getting close, and having trouble keeping the conversation going.

"Lou, are you doing it now?"

"No," I lied.

"Yes you are, I can tell," he replied.

"Sorry, you're right. All this talk was getting me going."

"Yeah, me too."

I could feel that Brad was also stroking off as we talked. I became bold in my movements. I couldn't respond right away, as I was busy spewing cum all over my tummy.

I could still feel Brad pumping himself. "You still there?" he asked. "It seems to have gotten quiet all of a sudden."

"Sorry, I was kind of distracted." I waited and a short silence met the end of the vibrations. "Brad?"

"Yeah..." he replied.

"You jerking off?"

"Just did."

"Me too."

"I know."

"Good night." And just like that, it was all over. I still found myself wondering what his cock looked like hard. How far and how much did he shoot? *I'm going to have to find out.*

* * *

The very next day, when I knew that Brad would be posted on duty, I shut the door to our room, stripped off my uniform, and began to think about Brad. I got out the hand lotion from my kit, and was really going at myself when I heard his footsteps approach the door. I quickly pulled up the sheet, barely covering my nakedness before he entered the room. "What the hell are you doing here?"

He shrugged and gave me a boyish smile. "I'm off duty now. I thought you might like to join me for some exercise."

Conscious of my own nakedness and my aroused state, I managed a shrug. "Well, maybe later."

"Oh, come on," Brad said, as he grabbed the sheet to pull it off. I struggled to keep covered, but his actions were faster, and I was suddenly very vulnerable. "Didn't you get enough last night?" Brad asked.

"Hey, buddy, there's no such thing as 'enough.'"

"Well, hurry up then," he said. I thought that he would leave the room, but he just walked over to his desk, facing the other way.

"Brad, uh...could you...leave?" I asked.

"Just do it, Lou. I won't watch," he replied. He sat down at the small desk and activated the computer.

He really isn't looking at me, I thought, *and I know that we both jerk off often enough with each other aware of it so what the hell!* I began to beat off again and I was so aroused that it only took a few minutes before I shot my load. As I gasped for breath, I saw that Brad had indeed been watching. "You pervert!" I said, unable to muster up any real anger at the situation.

"Not a bad show, Lou."

"Glad you liked it. You owe me one now," I joked. "Let me catch a quick shower and we're off."

"You're already off," Brad said, and then laughed.

"Cute," I smirked. I grabbed my towel and headed to the showers. On my return to our quarters, I was startled to see Brad lying on my bed, his grey pants around his hips, brown t-shirt shirt pulled up under his chin, beating himself off. I quickly closed the door but was unable to move.

"Sorry, hope you don't mind. I decided I needed a little relief too." Brad continued to pump his amazing cock as he talked to me.

My feet were glued to the deck, unable to move my eyes from his amazing cock. It was about seven inches, decent girth, tapered with a larger purple crown. Brad resumed his pumping and I felt my own dick swell under the white towel I was still wearing.

With a smile, Brad increased his speed, and was soon shooting cum onto his chest and tummy. "Could you hand me a cloth?" he asked after a moment.

"Yeah...sure." I could barely move my feet, but was able to hand him the box. I tried to respond like it was 'no big deal' and began to get my work-out clothes together. I dropped the towel to pull on my boxers.

"Thought you just took care of that," Brad relied, obviously in reference to my erection. He was sitting on the edge of the bed.

"Well, sometimes once is not enough," I replied, unable to admit that his little show had turned me on.

"You're a machine." Brad shook his head.

I just laughed it off.

* * *

We spent several hours working out and then took another shower. We soaped ourselves up, pointedly ignoring each other's naked bodies.

We were both in bed, after lights out, when Brad surprised me when he brought the topic up. "You put on a pretty good show earlier today. You've got a great dick."

I wasn't sure just how to respond. "Thanks...uh...you're not so bad yourself."

"I've never seen a guy jerk off before."

"No?" I asked in surprise. "You went through Basic didn't you?"

"They were more modest than you at Fort Chandlar." He shrugged. "It was pretty hot," he said, as if it were an admission of truth.

"You saw my reaction," I said.

"Are you doing *it* now?" Brad asked.

"Yes."

"Me too."

It was quiet for a minute. Suddenly, I heard Brad rustle around, and then his feet hit the floor. "Can I watch?" he asked.

"Yeah, sure."

He kneeled beside my bunk, naked. I could almost feel his breath on my skin. The glow of the light panels, set at night-level illumination, gave just enough light for him to watch. My arousal went through the roof, and his eyes provided all the stimulation I needed. Knowing this hot jock wanted to watch me was too much. I closed my eyes as I approached climax. When I opened my eyes, Brad was watching very closely as I shot my first volley of cum which hit my left cheek.

"Holy shit, man! You shot pretty far," he exclaimed.

I was suddenly very self-conscious of the cum, being naked, and feeling guilty. I reached for a tissue, and bumped into Brad. He saw what I was doing, and handed me the box. I was even more astounded when he leaned back on the floor, and began to beat off, obviously wanting me to watch. He spread his legs and played with his balls. I could hardly blink as he looked at me while increasing his tempo. It was only seconds before his breath caught in his throat, eyes rolled back in their sockets, and he shot ropes of cum all over his smooth chest. My heart was beating so fast from all the sexual energy that I could hear it in my ears. My erection had already returned.

Brad wiped off his chest, and stood to get into bed. His dick was only inches from my face, and I could smell his scent and cum as he jumped into bed.

I quickly, and quietly, brought myself to a second orgasm before falling asleep.

I knew we had crossed a line, and wasn't sure what to think or do. Brad's body was totally in my mind. I suddenly had thoughts of what it would be like to suck his cock, touch his balls, tongue his nipples. *Shit, would he be interested?*

Chapter Three

"We love the Guard."

The shout echoed from thirty throats as we charged down a corridor and through one of the hangers.

Technicians and sailors watched our platoon pass with amused grins.

I guess they didn't have to go through such training regimens. Daily exercise and training filled our days and sent us staggering back to our bunks at night for exhausted sleep.

"At least we only have to run in one gravity," Fred commented as we jogged down a corridor. "Back on the *Hellstar* we had to exercise under two gravities."

I groaned at the thought.

Fred laughed. "Captain Jorges said it would make men of us."

"Fuck that, Freddie."

"I didn't say I believed it, Brad, just that was what he thought."

"Then maybe I should have the gravity increased on this ship." Collin Duncan stepped around the corner and glared at us. "Did I tell any of you to stop running?" he asked us in a deceptively quiet voice.

"No, Sir!"

We broke into a fresh run.

* * *

A few nights later, I had an opportunity to ask Brad a question I had been wondering about for a while. "You ever had a blow job?"

"Yeah, lots of times. They're great. Why?"

"Oh, just wondered."

"Yeah, blow jobs are great, and so is fucking."

"Good head is hard to find. Some girls are better at it than others."

I paused for a moment. "I hear fags give the best head."

"I guess they would know just what men like. Sometimes I want to tell Cynthia to concentrate on the tip, just below the slit. That's where it feels best, right around the crown."

"I can just imagine how that would feel," I said.

"It's been too long for me. Jerking off is just not taking care of things too well."

"Hey, you're shaking the bed, buddy!" I joked.

"You're the one who got me thinking about blow jobs. You just shut up while I get off."

"My turn to watch then." I moved a chair closer to the bunk beds to stand on so that I could watch.

"Here is where the tongue feels like magic," Brad said, moving his cock to show me the place.

I moved closer to look. "Here?"

He took my hand and put my finger on the spot. I couldn't suppress my sharp intake of breath. *My hand was touching that beautiful cock.* I could feel the slipperiness of his pre-cum. I didn't pull away either, but began to explore. *I am not passing this chance up.*

The light was poor, so my face was close. I could smell him, his arousal obvious in his erection. Acting purely on lust, I touched his cock with my tongue. It was hot, hard, but velvet smooth.

Impulsively, I put my mouth over the crown, and Brad rolled his eyes back and groaned. "Shit, Lou, I'll give you a blow job if you do me."

"Deal." I didn't start off by going very deep, but had fun getting him all wet with saliva. The chair was awkward, and I couldn't get to his balls, but I managed to suck his hard cock enough, supplemented by hand strokes to get him off. I removed my mouth just before he shot and I could feel the pulse of his cum in my hand. He kept spilling more and more till I thought he would collapse.

"Fuck Lou." He sounded spent. "You're pretty good for a beginner."

"Oh, shut up." *He just has no idea.* I got back onto my bunk and waited for Brad. He got real close, and touched me first with his hand.

"I've never touched another cock before. It feels strange. You got pre-cum
on the tip."

"Just do it!" I demanded.

He was slow at first. His angle was much better, and he explored my balls and the region below. I groaned and began to push his head down for more.

"Hey, take it easy, I'm about to choke. I'll get you off."

I could feel my hips rise and fall with his suction. I became more frantic as I approached climax. My groans were pretty loud as I shot the first volley. Brad was surprised, and quickly withdrew his mouth, dripping cum. The second volley hit him square in the face and hair. He used his hand to ensure I was finished. "Why didn't you warn me?" he asked.

"I thought you could tell. My butt was so far off the mattress, I was sure you knew what was next. Man, that was fucking incredible." I smiled to myself as I watched Brad clean off his face. His cock was swinging as he stood up to climb back into his bunk. I reached out and tugged on it, and as if it were a person. "Good night."

* * *

The following morning came too soon.

I finally had to get out of bed.

Brad was still asleep, so I quietly got up and used the bathroom. On return, I sat in my desk chair, and couldn't help notice how handsome Brad looked as he lay on his side. His thin white sheet was barely covering his body. His back was exposed as well as half of his ass. His face was so innocent. His eye opened, and he smiled.

"Good morning," I said.

"I could feel your eyes," Brad said, as he yawned.

"Sorry, you just looked so innocent and pure in the morning light."

"Don't feel very innocent," he said, as he swung his legs over the side of the bed. His morning erection very evident under his grey boxer shorts.

"Well, now you look very devilish."

"I feel pretty devilish," he said, touching his erection, spreading his legs ever so slightly. "Looks like your devil is waking up too."

I could feel my own passion rising at the visual display before me. My own

boxer shorts had an obvious tenting effect. My hand moved downwards with a will of it's own, searching for pleasure. Under my waist-band, my hand began to bring pleasure to my body. Brad was tweaking his nipple with his second hand.

I stood and slipped off my shorts, sitting back down on the very edge of the chair. My legs were spread as I began to explore my body. The sexual energy in the room was almost smothering out the oxygen.

Brad made continued eye contact, only disrupted by his interest in my cock. He manipulated his balls, and several fingers disappeared to regions below.

My cock was aching with need. My eyes were suddenly glued on Brad's

rigid cock. As if being manipulated by puppet strings, I arose and moved over to him. Sitting on the bunk bed put me at a perfect height to watch him masturbate. I had never seen him so closely in the light of day, and could see the veins engorged with blood. A clear drop appeared at the tip, and I moved closer to take it with my tongue.

Brad immediately withdrew his hand. "Yeah, Lou, suck it. You're the best cock-sucker I've ever met."

His words were like magic, and my mouth became a sexual organ. I concentrated on that spot below the slit. I could only get about half of his shaft in my mouth. I suddenly shifted to his balls, taking them one by one. I lifted them to explore the regions below. I could hear Brad moan louder as my tongue touched and moved. He brought his knees to the edge of the bed, which made my job easier. His rosebud was suddenly visible. I moved my finger to touch him there, and he seemed even more aroused. Using saliva, I began to circle the muscle ring, while continuing stimulating the perineum with my tongue. Brad pushed his ass at me, in an obvious attempt to increase his stimulation. Adding more spit, I pushed the finger past the resistance. I pushed the finger inside, and began to explore. The musky scent was overwhelming, and I could feel my own cock ache with need.

Brad's cock was pushed against his tummy, and I brought it towards my lips. Brad sat more upright, putting pressure on my probing finger. The amount of pre-cum surprised me as I spread it around the tip with my tongue. The flavour was more pronounced, slightly salty and silky smooth. I kept the hand in place as I began to apply suction to the upper half. My eyes were open, watching his obvious pleasure as his face began to contort with his approaching orgasm.

I first felt his ass muscles constrict against my finger. I pressed deeper, and increased my pace of my sucking. His cock expanded seconds before I tasted his first eruptions. The powerful spurts choked me with their force, and I withdrew only to be hit in the face with the next splash of cum. The visual stimulation was intense, a sight I would relive for many months in my own personal fantasy. After three or four more contractions and splashes of cum, I took him back in my mouth. The flavour was bland, but intensely Brad, and I continued to suck till he softened. I used my finger to harvest all the semen I could from my face. I sucked my finger like a miniature cock.

"Fuck, that was awesome."

I smiled. "Glad you liked it." My cock was demanding relief, almost aching with need.

"Man, that was fucking fantastic. I've never had anyone pay any attention to my ass like that before. I didn't know that could feel so wonderful. You sit on my bed, and I'll see what I can do for you."

I lost no time, but found it difficult to climb onto the upper bunk. I felt

Brad's hand on my ass, pushing me up. I sat on the edge, and saw Brad smile as he brought his mouth to my cock. He swirled his tongue around the crown, and smiled at me. He quickly engulfed my smaller dick, almost to the base.

In a few strokes, I began to feel myself getting close. It was as if he knew this as he shifted to my balls. I spread my legs as he rolled them around in his mouth. He pulled me closer to the edge as he moved lower. I leaned back, and could feel the cool air on my ass. I was nervous, feeling very vulnerable in this position but I could feel his tongue on that special place.

Unable to see, I soon felt his fingertip press against my ass. I suddenly wanted to be dominated by Brad, completely lost in my trust for him. His finger made several attempts, and after a fresh coating of saliva, entered me. The pain was only slight, and I felt him move inside. He touched a part inside, and I felt my whole body respond. With no direct touch, I felt my orgasm suddenly explode.

The spurt of cum hit the wall behind me. Brad quickly grabbed my cock, and the second blast hit him in the face before he could get me inside his mouth. I felt his warmth surround my cock, as I finished the most intense orgasm of my life. My body felt like jelly as he withdrew his mouth from my limp cock. Words could not describe the pleasure I had just experience, nor the love I felt for Brad at that moment.

"I need a shower after that," I heard him say. I collapsed onto his bed and could smell his scent on his pillow. Completely safe and secure, I fell asleep.

I awoke as Brad was dressing. "Hey, get up. The day's almost half over."

"Liar." I couldn't have slept so long.

Chapter Four

"*Action stations*!" a voice crackled over the intercom even as the harsh shriek of the alert siren warned everyone on board that the ship was being boarded by hostile soldiers. "*All personnel to battle stations. Marine detachments report to deck five.*"

I hastily pulled on my body armour. Ferro-ceramic vest and helmet. Hot and sweaty to wear, even with the cooling Kevlar jumpsuit underneath it. But it would help keep me alive on the battlefields, so it was worth wearing.

The men of my squad formed up.

Corporal Earl Cheney nodded as he surveyed us. "We have our orders," he informed us. "Deck five, section three. Near forward fire control."

I was familiar with the location from my training. A vital installation for the *Vindication* if the frigate was to continue fighting the larger battle. *If they take Fire Control, they can stop us from shooting...or open fire on friendly ships. We can't allow that.*

"Move out. Weapons are clear to fire." Earl gestured. "Watch out for the ship's crew. I don't want friendly fire incidents."

We ran, our boots thudding loudly on the deck.

The intercom was chattering continuously with updated damage reports and word of multiple hull breaches.

The ceiling light panels flickered and most of them went dark.

"Keep moving!" Earl shouted. "You should know this ship like that the feel of your dick!"

Our endless training runs were making more sense now. We did know this layout of the frigate, lights or no lights.

Figures moved in the corridor ahead.

"Intruders spotted!" someone called out.

Gunfire erupted and a hail of bullets splattered across the bulkheads.

"Shit!"

I saw Earl go down, multiple impacts marking red on his chest.

Brad took cover in a half-open access panel and fired a burst from his *Wesson Rattler* machine gun. Return fire narrowly missed him.

I dove to the deck, and fired my own *Rattler*.

"Fucking A!" Fred shouted from somewhere behind me.

Bullets whined past my face. I kissed deck-plates and kept shooting.

A fresh hail of gunfire whined down the corridor.

Someone screamed as he died.

"We can't hold them. We gotta fall back!"

"No, we gotta hold this corridor." Brad hosed the far end of the corridor. "We don't fall back until the Major orders it." He snapped a fresh clip into his gun.

I squeezed off a pair of shots. *Am I hitting anything?* There was no way to tell of course.

Fred pushed forward, firing as he went. "We can take 'em."

Another burst of fire answered him. Bullets ricocheted past my head.

The rattle of fire died down.

I looked around. "We held."

Brad nodded. "Barely." He and I were the only survivors.

"Not a bad training session."

Corporal Earl stood at the end of his line. The red splatters of paint on his armour clearly showed his *demise*.

"You managed to blunt the invaders," Major Duncan continued. Unlike us, he did not appear out-of-breath, nor was his hair sweaty and mussed. "With the protection of fire control, the *Vindication* was able to destroy the next wave of assault shuttles."

"I trust that we will match this success in a real battle," Earl replied.

"It can be hoped that you do not suffer so many casualties in the process. Two survivors out of eight is not good enough." Collin Duncan frowned. "Not good enough at all."

"With all respect, how often does a warship get boarded?" I asked. *Civies for sure, but who would got after a warship?*

"You don't have permission to speak!" Earl snapped at me.

"It doesn't happen often," Collin told me, after a look. "But in case it does, I don't want to be the officer who let the rebels gain control of a warship."

We waited silently.

"The drills will continue." He turned. "Corporal Fischer, what did you learn from this?"

"We moved too slowly," he replied. His hair was still sweaty and messed up from his helmet. He had led the simulated boarding party. Like the rest of his squad, his armour was marked with red paint.

"Yes, you did." Collins nodded. "You moved too slow and allowed the defenders to seize a choke point and tie you down."

"We had reinforcements coming."

"They were tied down as well." His dark eyes flicked to the other marines. "Even if you had eliminated the last two defenders, the rest of the marines would have closed in on you."

"Yes, Sir."

"Take notes on this," Collins announced. "Next time the roles will be reversed and you can try the other side's mission."

"Oh goodie," Fred muttered. "Vacumn duty."

Duncan ignored him. "Dismissed."

Chapter Five

We were assigned to New Wessex for several months after our initial training missions.

The Rebellion was heating up and the Guard was being readied for new assignments.

I had been in the military for about nearly two years by then. I had progressed through the low ranks fairly quickly, having started as PFC—private first class—as opposed to most cadets who started as PV1 or PV2—buck privates. I was just conferred in my rank as corporal when the company was sent three new recruits.

The *Truculent Lancers* had been split up and my company was stationed on the surface. It wasn't a bad world, fairly temperate climate, and our garrison was stationed near the capitol. Being an officer, however low-ranking, I was placed in command of one squad.

There was this one recruit who had just arrived from the core worlds and his name was Jeff. With his blond-hair, blue-eyes, square-jaw, and slender build, he was the cutest thing I had ever seen in my days in the military. And I knew from the first moment that I saw him that I wanted him. Little did I know that he wanted me too.

We were introduced, and I took a paternal instinctive stance with Jeff, in that he was new meat, and needed to be protected from the more seasoned soldiers. They were apt to be too hard on him, due to his lack of on the job experience. So, I tried to lighten the atmosphere by asking Jeff if he liked Greek food, since there was a nice Greek restaurant nearby, where I liked to go once in a while. "Reminds me of home," I told him.

He confided that he had never tried Greek food, but would like to try it, and so off we went. We had an enjoyable meal, and then talked a lot together during and afterwards. We found out that we liked each other, and Jeff hinted that he liked me quite a bit, and would like to get to know me more intimately.

I was intrigued, and told him to come to my quarters later in the evening for a beer, or something. He accepted and said he would be there. Private quarters were a real luxury and I enjoyed having privacy...though I also missed having a bunk-mate. Brad had been assigned to the garrison over on Sandhurst. *"The Guard has no respect for a man's sex life,"* he had cursed when the transfer orders arrived. *"Still, it should just be temporary."*

I sat up and waited in a pair of tight running shorts, reading a book. Jeff knocked on my door, and I let him in.

After looking down the hallway to see if any one noticed his coming to my room—and not seeing anyone—I shut the door, and clicked the lock. He smiled and sat on the bed.

"Nice room, you are lucky. I have three other guys sharing my room," he told me.

I sat next to him on the bedside. "We can talk here without anyone else overhearing. Or would you rather not talk?" Putting my hand gently on his lap, I began to massage the rather large bulge that was obviously growing larger with each minute. "Your choice."

Jeff reached over and took me in him arms and kissed me without warning. That was really unexpected!

I stood up and hurried to the window. I shut the curtains tightly, and told him to remain silent as I went over to the door and shut off the light switch. "Try to be really quiet buddy, we wouldn't want to get in trouble tonight," I whispered in Jeff's ear, and then allowed my tongue to gently probe his smooth ear.

Jeff squirmed and then wrapped his arms tightly around my body. He was still in those damned camouflage pants and grey tee-shirt. I was so used to seeing those stupid uniforms all day long that I didn't want this hot stud to be in it while we were together.

"Jeff, why don't you get comfortable. We're all alone. You can take that uniform off, can't you?"

He smiled and then nodded. Taking his tee-shirt off and exposing his smooth chest and sensuously erotic brown nipples got hard just looking at him.

I motioned to him to step towards me. I took him in my arms and let my tongue stray over his sexy nipples flicking it over each one until they were both very hard. He was breathing faster now, and his pants were tenting upwards. I undid the five buttons down the front and slid his pants down. He kicked off his now-unlaced boots, and was standing before me dressed only in his briefs and socks. I reached down and slid the socks off of him, and then stood up next to him as we both pulled each others' pants off.

Our now naked bodies were touching, and our cocks were so damned hard I couldn't wait another second to have him. He was very sensual, and took his time though.

"I don't want just a quick fuck," Jeff told me. "I want to enjoy the night." His hands gently caressed the globes of my ass, his fingers probed my ass-crack as I stared into his beautiful brown eyes and I melted. Jeff was built like a runner, his body was lithe, and his legs were strong and muscular. His chest was smooth and well developed with strong biceps and triceps to compliment his whole frame. He wasn't hung like a horse, but he wasn't small in any way either. His cock was firm and about seven inches long, and not really thick...a perfect mouthful though. The entire area was surrounded with silky blond pubic hair nesting his balls which my fingers were now caressing. My lips pressed against Jeff's and our tongues entered each others' mouths. They explored the inner areas of our mouths and lapped gently over one another. My hand wrapped around his rock hard cock and stroked gently. He moaned softly—remembering where we were—and I began to slide down kissing his neck and shoulders. Licking his beautiful nipples again, and running my tongue down the crevice of his stomach to his navel, rimming the cute button of his stomach and trailing even lower as my hands massaged his legs and feet.

I aimed at my target, the beautiful object of my desire: his meaty cock, standing at attention waiting for me to take him into ecstacy. I wasn't going to hold back any more. So I plunged onto that cock opening my mouth as wide as possible, taking in as much as possible without gagging. I took the whole thing into my mouth as my nose pressed into his blond pubic hair. I could smell how clean he was, the smell of freshly washed hair right under my nose. His cock tasted good too, also clean and fresh—but distinctly like Jeff.

Jeff's hips thrust upwards to meet the sucking action of my mouth...I pressed his chest down to let him know that I could do it without help...he relaxed and let me do the sucking. I let my mouth glide over his cock gently making his body shake up and down. He was enjoying my work, and wanted to reciprocate...he slid me around and took my balls into his mouth, and lapped at them making me tingle. Soon he took my cock deep into his mouth and showed me that he could suck cock like a pro. I was feeling so good that I didn't realize that he was getting close, when I got a spurt of pre-cum on my tongue, and I savoured the precious liquid then swallowed it. I began to pay more attention to the hot stud's cock I was sucking on, and awaited the hot payload I was about to get.

Jeff was still running his fingers up and down my ass-crack and finally began to probe my asshole. It felt real good, and so I started to suck him a bit faster to signal that I was enjoying it. He reached up and took the tube of K-Y that I had pulled out of my desk drawer earlier, and greased his index finger with it generously. My body pulsed in joy as his finger entered my asshole! He knew right where my prostate was! He massaged it and I sucked like there was no tomorrow...I moaned with his cock deep in my throat as I shot what must have been a huge load down his throat, which he swallowed quickly and licked up as I felt his cock get stiffer and throb in my mouth. I prepared myself for the hot blast of cum that was to fill my mouth twice. I drank his cum deep into my throat and then we hugged each other for hours and then fell asleep.

Luckily it was a weekend, or we would've had a lot of trouble. Jeff woke up first, and was coming back into the room from the shower—he was the cleanest guy I'd ever met—and then climbed back in bed. In a matter of seconds we were on each other again.

* * *

Officially we were on patrol.

Unofficially we were driving around the countryside, watching for any suspicious activity.

Jeff looked amazing in his grey uniform and I enjoyed allowing him to take the lead...so that I could admire his tight ass. We kept finding deserted corners and alleys where we could stop and kiss. We were seriously making out at every chance we could steal.

After a little more kissing, cuddling, and sucking, I convinced Jeff to come back to my quarters again.

He rode with me in my jeep, and it was all I could do to keep on the road as I steered with one hand and rubbed his crotch with the other. It didn't take us long to reach my apartment, as I had been driving like a fucking maniac in my frenzy to

get this boy to my bed.

We went inside, and I offered him a drink. "Beer would be good," he said. As I took two cold ones from the fridge, he said he had to take a piss.

"Can I watch?" I asked.

"No!" he replied, surprised that I would even ask such a thing. I myself was surprised that he wouldn't let me, but he said he got "stage fright" if anyone watched, and he couldn't pee. So I allowed him this little privacy, knowing that I would get another look at that cock soon enough.

We wandered over to the bed and took a couple of big gulps of brew, and set aside the bottles. I removed his shirt and cap, playing with his lovely chest and tummy a bit before lowering his trousers. Once his pants were off, I once again relished the sight of him in his lily white boxers which contrasted nicely with his tan.

"Did you ever fool around with the other guys in your barracks?" I asked him.

"No," he instantly replied. "I don't do queer things like that."

I had to hide my smile. He was handing me a load of complete bull shit, but this was also exactly what I wanted to hear: he was a straight boy who had never had sex with another guy but had always wanted to.

After tickling his cock through the linen of his shorts and gently stroking

his pubic hair through the open fly, I pulled the shorts down to reveal once more that magnificent object of my desire. I bent over and briefly, lightly kissed his cock-head, and then quickly shed all my clothes. I led him over to the bed, where we lay down side by side and started to French kiss, our bodies pressed together, each of our rock-hard dicks pressing insistently against the other's tummy. We lay there for a good long while, just kissing and stroking, as if we were lovers. At that moment, I indeed did love this boy more than anyone else in the world, even though I hardly knew him at all.

Chapter Six

"Charge."

I ducked as bullets whined past my head.

"Training missions. I hate these fucking things." Mikael was behind a crate as a fresh wave of bullets pelted around us.

"What should we do?"

"See any targets?"

"No."

"Great."

I could see figures moving past a parked loader. "Over there!" I squeezed off a few shots. *I wonder if Jeff is among them?* He had been assigned to act as aggressors in the combat simulation. *At least I think he's been assigned to the terrorists. He could be part of another security detail.* Major Collin liked to keep things complicated.

"Watch for civilians," Earl warned us over the comm.

"Civilians?" Freddie shook his head. "What the fuck would civilians be doing in a firefight?" He snapped off a few shots at some target he thought he saw.

"Be the kind of thing Collin would send in to mess up our simulation."

"Yeah, he likes screwing with us."

"He needs to be screwed."

"You volunteering, Mikael?"

"Shut up."

"Targets down," Earl called out. "Squad move up. Check for survivors."

"Copy that."

I crept forward, my *Rattler* held at the ready.

* * *

New Wessex was a fairly peaceful colony. There was no evidence of any active rebellion and our garrison was more of a staging point for missions further into the rim territories.

I decided to head into Jamestown one day, in full uniform. The streets were crowded with civilians. I decided that I needed to spend some time amongst the faceless crowds.

A trio of Centurion tanks rumbled past me as I headed towards the vehicle pool. The armoured tanks were slow and massive, with enough firepower to level half a city block. *Not that there was any reason to deploy them on this world,* I thought. *New Wessex is too peaceful.* My lips twitched in a smile. *Those three tanks alone have more firepower than the entire planetary police force.*

For some reason, driving the jeep from the base made me horny. Probably came from thinking about Jeff. *Why did he have to get reassigned to orbital duty?* I wondered as I drove. *Some marines never get transferred between squads and yet every squad I am in gets broken up. Usually just when I get a new guy properly broken in.* There was a serious swelling in the front of my pants and it ended up with me driving along the highway with my dick getting harder and harder.

And then I saw the *Construction Ahead* and *Watch for Flagman* signs along the roadside and then a long line of cars, all stopped. *Shit*, I thought, *just my luck*. I stopped the jeep, shut off the engine and tried to ease my dick around in my pants, to relieve the pressure.

Finally I just unbuttoned my pants, pushed my *Jockeys* down and let it out, into the air. As soon as I did, it went full hard so I dug my balls out, to give them some breathing room. *What a great sensation.* A little breeze was blowing through the window, cooling my hard dick and ruffling the long, silky hairs on my balls. I wanted to save my cum for the post-poker game blow-out later than night so I didn't jack off, just played with my nuts and rubbed the base of my dick a little.

After five minutes or so I spotted one of the construction workers slowly making his way along the line of cars, talking to each of the drivers. My jeep sat fairly high so I figured he'd never see what I was doing.

"Sorry for the delay, guy." He was wearing one of those bright orange

vests, the kind highway guys have to wear for safety, but his chest was bare and I could see sweat in the curly brown hair that covered his pecs. He looked dusty, too.

"No problem. What's going on?"

"Paving up ahead. Always rough on the traffic but we should be able to

open one lane pretty soon. Say," he continued, looking up at the jeep, "I've never seen a military model up close before. Mind if I take a quick look?"

Before I could answer, he'd hopped up on the running board and was looking in. "Nice." When he saw my hard dick sticking out of my pants, he did a quick double take, then gave out a low, lewd whistle. "Whoa! Looks like yer seriously overheatin'. Where you headed??"

I shrugged. "Over to Bayside. You know, the park."

The car in front of me started up and began to move so he jumped down. "Well, be careful with that thing 'til you get there," he joked. Then he walked away with a wave.

I eyed a couple of hot-looking local guys as I took a walk along the river, but they took no real notice of me. *Damn, they only see the uniform.*

Finally I gave it up and headed back to the barracks.

There was supposed to be a wild poker game and I had high hopes of how it would turn out.

The road crew had quit for the day by the time I reached that part of the highway and I sailed right through the construction zone. About a mile further I saw one of the guys, still wearing his orange vest, walking alongside the road. I pulled over to see if I could give him a lift. When he came up to the jeep I recognized him from earlier.

"Sure, thanks a lot." He smiled—it made him look really cute. "My own car's in the garage up there," he pointed up the road, towards the next town. "Supposed to be ready by now."

"No problem then. It's on my way back to base."

He brushed the dust off his *Levi's* as best he could and climbed into the jeep. "The name's Liam," he said, holding out his hand. "I really appreciate this."

"Lou."

"A member of the Marines I see."

"Ready to serve." I shrugged.

"The garage is just off the next turn."

"Okay." I pulled in.

When Liam came out of the office he looked fit to be tied. "Goddamn son-of-a-bitch! Had to order a part and wouldn't you know, it won't be here, maybe for a couple of days. Now what the hell am I supposed to do?"

"Walk to work?"

"Screw that. I'll just have to arrange a ride with a buddy." Liam frowned. "So I guess it's off to the house then."

"That far?" I asked him.

"Just up the road."

"I've brought you this far. Hop in."

"Thanks, Lou. You're a real gentleman." Liam climbed back into the jeep.

When we got to the house it seemed hotter even than it had been out on the road, so we grabbed a couple of brews and hit the pool.

I took a look at Liam's equipment as he pulled his clothes off; it seemed only fair since he'd gotten a pretty good look at mine that afternoon. He was uncut, and maybe had a slight edge on me in the size department. His dick was shaped like a bat, thin at the base and then flaring out into a thick tube. The head was completely hidden by a cowl of smooth, pink skin. With a hefty piece like that, along with thick brown hair covering his chest and belly, I figured he got just about any woman he wanted.

We splashed around in the pool for a while and then lay on the deck, drinking our beer.

"So how was the park?"

"Peaceful. Quiet."

"We're not a rebellious world. No sparks here." He turned. "Or are there?"

"Sparks?"

"Yeah...Lou, like when you tease your nipples. Makes your nipples all hard and shoots sparks off in your balls, you know?"

"I'm not sure about that."

"You're kidding!" Liam pulled himself up on his arm, lookin' at me. "It's instant hard-on."

"I doubt that," I said. "Nothing's instant hard-on."

Liam didn't say anything, but the next thing I knew he'd leaned forward and was gently twisting my left nipple . When he took my other tit in his hand, rolling it between his thumb and forefinger, I guess I just sorta groaned. A second or so later he pulled back and began to chuckle. "Now do you believe me?"

I followed his eyes down to my dick, which was sticking straight up from my belly, rock hard.

"You want some more?"

Shit, why not, I thought. "Fuck yeah."

Liam leaned over and licked at my nipples, first one, then the other. The sparks began to fire off in my balls and I felt my dick begin to throb. When I reached out and grabbed one of his nipples he gasped and bit down a little. My dick jerked and I heard it smack against my belly.

"You like that, Liam?"

He moaned, deep in his throat. "God, yes. Work on my tits and I'll do anything." His mouth went back to my chest.

"Anything?" I felt him nod against me. I pinched his nipple again and when he groaned, well, it just slipped out—I heard myself mutter: "Suck me. Suck my dick."

He twisted himself around so I could hang onto his tits; then I felt his tongue on my dick, wet and hot. He licked across the swollen head a couple of times, then started at the base, lapping at the whole length till it was slick all over. Then he slapped the head into his mouth and held it there with his lips, his tongue poking at the pee slit. When he skimmed his tongue over that little bundle of skin on the underside, just below the head, I jerked and sucked in my breath. At the same time

I guess I pinched hard on both his tits because he let out a loud moan and suddenly swallowed my whole dick, right down to the root. He stayed that way for a bit, his nose pressed into my hairy balls; then he slowly raised up till just the head of my dick was in his mouth.

We rolled onto our sides and he sucked my dick back into his mouth, letting his tongue wander over the shaft. It was funny but I found I could control him with his tits. The harder I squeezed and pinched, the deeper he slid down on my dick; when I gently rolled them between my fingers he moved up, flicking his tongue around the head.

I opened my eyes and realized Liam's dick was level with my face. I let go of one of Liam's tits, reached up and gripped his dick. It felt hot and jerked in my hand. I was surprised how easily the foreskin slipped back over the head, almost like it was greased. It bunched up behind the head, then slid forward again. When I pulled it back tight, it stayed there and his dick looked circumcised, like mine.

Liam's cock got harder than mine, didn't have the thick veins mine does. I found myself wondering what it would taste like. I stuck my tongue out, just to touch it, but Liam thrust his hips and I suddenly had the whole thing in my mouth. It tasted kind of salty at first, and a little bit sweet. I ran my tongue around the head, flicking back and forth. It seemed to drive him crazy. I held his dick in my mouth for some time, swirling my tongue over it. All the while, the pressure was mounting down in my balls. I knew I wasn't good for much longer; what Liam was doing was going to bring me off any second. I tried to signal him but he just shoved his dick deeper into my mouth. Pretty soon it was too late. My cock exploded and I began to pump blasts of cum into Liam's throat, howling around the dick in my mouth. The feeling was so good I didn't realize Liam was cumming too, and I was swallowing it! It tasted funny, not like anything I recognized. Liam

kept thrusting his hips, almost like he was fucking, and I had to keep swallowing.

When it was all over I just lay there, wondering what had happened.

Finally Liam sat up. "My God that was good." He looked at me. "You okay, Lou?"

"Fuck yeah." I rolled over and dropped into the pool.

When I came up Liam was standing at the edge, laughing.

"What's so damn funny, Liam?"

"Nothing. You hungry?"

"Yeah."

"I've got some steaks we can have."

I dropped my towel and started to get dressed. "Sounds great."

"Skip the clothes. I like the way you look when you're naked. The way you walk."

"What do you mean, the way I walk? I walk the same, naked or..."

"Oh, no you don't. When you're naked you strut; you make your dick swing between your legs, like you're proud of that big meat. And you should be; you really look good naked."

Somehow, that pleased me. I mean, I know I have a strong, hard body and

a fairly big dick. And it sure felt good strutting around. "Okay, but only if you stay bare-assed too."

"Deal."

Liam rooted around in his freezer and found some fries to cook while I made a salad and Liam grilled the steaks. We ate out on the deck and after ward took our beers and went down by the pool again. I pulled a couple of pads off the lounges and we lay down, looking at the stars and sucking our brews.

"Do you see your ship?"

"No." I studied the sky. There were some lights moving quickly across the night sky, but I thought they were just satellites.

After a few minutes Liam reached over and began playing with my nipples

again. Just like before, it set off sparks in my balls and within ten seconds I'd sprung a rod. "Are we gonna do it again?" I asked, reaching for his nipple. The moon had come up and I could see that Liam was as hard as me.

He didn't answer right away, just concentrated on my chest. Finally he said, "Yeah. But not the same."

"Not the same? What..." Liam pinched my nipples hard and I forgot what I was going to say, cause it felt so good. Then his hand dropped down and he started playing with my balls.

"Fuck," Liam said, quietly.

"Huh?"

"Fuck. We're gonna fuck." He rolled away from me and found his jeans, dug around in them for a bit and then lay down again. He had a rubber in his hand. "Come up here," he said, pulling me onto his chest. Very slowly he sucked my hard dick into his mouth, his hands on my ass cheeks, pulling me closer until my balls were on his chin. After a long time he pushed me back a little, so he could get some air, and let his tongue roam over my dick. After a while he slid me further back, until I could feel something poking at my ass. I knew, then, what he wanted. I was so horny and turned on that I wanted it too, but that thing of his was so damn big....

I reached behind me. It felt huge. "I don't think I can, Liam."

"Sure you can. You just gotta do it slowly." He started working on my tits again. "Let yourself relax and open up."

He'd put on a condom and when I took a deep breath, the head of his dick just slipped into me, like a well oiled piston into its sleeve. I thought there should be some pain but there wasn't, just a strange feeling of fullness as I slowly settled onto his dick. I sank down until I felt his wiry hair against my ass. We stayed like that for a couple of minutes, not saying anything. Then Liam let out a deep sigh and pushed me over until I was lying on my back with my legs over his.

"Easy, Liam. Please."

"I will." He pulled back a little, his dick sliding part way out of me. Then he pushed back in. He did it again but with a longer stroke, faster. On the third one he hit something up inside me and I let out a groan. "You okay, Lou?"

"Yeah, except that I'm gonna cum pretty quick. Especially if you do that again."

"What?"" He stroked again and hit the same place, harder. "That?"

I groaned again. "Yeah, that!" I felt my dick leaking all over my belly like a little fountain.

"Well then...." He began to fuck me, slowly at first, then getting faster, punching in and out. I closed my eyes and worked my ass muscles on his dick, clamping down as he pulled out, opening up as he shoved himself back in. My balls tightened up into my crotch; I knew I couldn't last much longer. Didn't seem like he would, either.

When he slammed his dickhead against that place up inside me, it was all over. We both let go and I felt his cock blasting inside me; I hollered and spewed my load out between us, shooting volley after volley, spraying us both.

We rolled onto our sides and lay still for a bit, catching our breath.

"Fuck, that was nice."

"Yeah." I felt his dick begin to go soft in me. He sighed, easing it out, leaving my ass with a strange empty feeling.

Liam handed me my beer. "We gonna get embarrassed about this, too?"

"Seems pointless now." I took a slug of my now-warm beer. "I will be pretty disappointed, though, if you don't have a couple more of those rubbers in your pocket."

He smiled.

Chapter Seven

Part of my military duties in while stationed on New Wessex was to escort valuable military supplies from the *Vindication* to a depot on the coast of one of the islands. I spent a lot of time flying back and forth in a C-130 military cargo shuttle. Most of the time these trips were long, noisy, hot, and boring. But one trip did prove a memorable exception.

Many of the C.G.. flight crews were reservists who had been called to active duty during the Outer Worlds Rebellion. On this particular flight, the crew were a bunch of good old boys out of New Houston. The "Load" or senior cargo handler was a big strapping Tech Sergeant from some backwater planet. He was handsome in a rugged way and had an easy, friendly manner. I soon learned that the crew called him Norm, which was short for Norman.

Norm and I got along instantly. He loved to swap bullshit stories and really ate up my off-color "no-shit" C.G.. tales. If you've never been in the service, you may not appreciate the collection of stories that we accumulate. Since, I had been in the service for nearly a decade, I had a shit-load of war stories.

The first leg of our flight went by pretty quickly. We landed at about

midnight at some non-descript civilian field to refuel and the C-130 immediately developed an oil leak. Norm told me that it would be at least ten hours before the shuttle was ready to fly again. This was bad news since I had to stay with the cargo that was loaded on the shuttle. Military supplies have a tendency to disappear when not being constantly watched.

The whole crew, plus Norm took off and left me with the shuttle. I decided to make the best of it and curled up in my sleeping bag and went to sleep. There are two things that a soldier never gets enough of: sleep and sex. I was determined to spend the next ten hours catching up on my sleep.

A short time later, Norm woke me up.

"Is it time to go?" I asked.

"No, I thought that you might want some company," he replied.

Norm had stripped off his navy blue flight suit and was wearing only a pair of grey flannel running shorts. The mat of dark brown hair that covered the stud's thickly muscled chest caught my immediate attention. I would have loved to run my fingers through his hairy chest pelt.

I was wearing only a pair of boxer shorts, since I didn't want to wrinkle my normal duty fatigues. Norm quickly noticed that I had an early morning hard-on. I must have had an interesting dream but damned if could remember what it had been. The closeness of this handsome stud from the hills drove out all other thoughts.

Norm noticed the hard cock sticking out of the fly of my boxer shorts. A drop of clear fluid was dripping from the piss hole. That sure must have been one hot dream that I was having.

"I was wondering were I left that crow-bar," Norm said as he stared at my hard prick.

"Yeah, I guess the hard fucker got a little lonely out here."

"Well, perhaps I got something that can keep him company," he said and quickly stripped off his shorts.

What a sight! Norm had at least eight and a half inches of the nicest looking cock that I had seen in some time. Norm ran his hands over my hairy chest and said, "You're one hot fucking stud, Lou."

"You're quite a good looking stud yourself, Norm!" I replied.

I reached and grabbed a handful of Norm's massive tool and worked the tight folds of foreskin carefully back over the thick head of his cock. I have always found uncut cocks to be a real turn on especially when attached to studs as hunky as Norm.

Norm knelt over me, bringing our cocks together. I took both hard, hairy shafts into my hand and began to stroke them together. I loved the feel of his hard, man pole gripped tightly next to my own throbbing fucker. The feel and smell of his masculine body had me really turned on. Even though it was night in the desert, we were both quickly covered with a sheen of musky smelling sweat. The fresh smell of man sweat only added to the enjoyment of the moment.

Norm breathed deeply several times enjoying the sensation of our shared jack off. He ground his sweaty body against me, moaning with excitement.

Although I enjoyed the feel of Norm's body next to mine, I wanted to do more than jack off with this virile hunk. I was hoping that he also had something else in mind.

Norm sure did have some ideas. He pulled his dick out of my hand and bent over my crotch and swallowed my hard cock to the base. I shuddered as the tight ring of his hot, wet lips quickly descended down the shaft of my throbbing poker to the hairy base of my prick. I could tell that my cock wasn't the first prick that this Air Guard stud had ever inhaled into his wet mouth.

"Take that dick! Suck that hard cock down you throat."

Norm held my cock deep within his throat for a moment, and then began to suck in earnest. On each up stroke he would swirl his talented tongue along the sensitive underside of my cock head. On the down strokes, he would butt his forehead gently against my hairy belly. This country boy sure knew how to give one hell of a hot blowjob.

Norm worked intently and noisily on the jutting tower of flesh that rose

from my groin until the sensation became just too much for me. I was on the brink, but wanted to take my time with this hot fucking stud. I grabbed him firmly by his broad shoulders and brought his bobbing head to a halt. "Hold, on fella. I just about shot my wad," I explained breathlessly.

Norm released my saliva soaked cock from his talented mouth and smiled at me, his blue eyes sparkling with lust. Pumping my hard shaft in his tightly clenched hand he asked: "Okay, what's next?"

I thought long and hard about my reply. Norm was one hell of a good-looking stud. I ran my hands through the dense, sweaty mat of hair covering his hard chest. "Every once in a while I let the right guy get a shot at my asshole."

"And do you think that I'm the right guy?" he asked with a smile.

"I'm positive that you are the right guy to give me a hard cock up the ass," I replied earnestly. I had only let a few other men get a shot at my ass, but I was homier than hell and Norm was exactly the type of well built and virile military stud and could get me hot enough to want and try it. I knew that the hard length of cock was going to hurt at first but I was willing to try.

"It will be easier on the bench seat," Norm told me, indicating the pull down cargo seats used for passengers on the C-130. I stood up and lay back on one of the bench seats, my legs handing over the edge. I wanted to be on my back so I could watch this stud fuck my eager ass.

"That's it guy, put those fucking legs up. I want to really get this cock into your hot ass," he instructed. The pilot was hot and horny; the good naturedness turned into lust filled passion. Horny need had replaced civility. I didn't mind; I wanted this stud to fuck me, any way he wanted.

Norm must have come out to the plane ready for action. When he spread my ass cheeks and placed the head of his uncut cock against me, he was already slick and greasy. The blunt head of his cock pushed gently but firmly against my anus, entering slowly into the tight ring. I tried to relax, to make his penetration easier, but his cock was so fucking big. Slowly my anal ring gave way and the head of his cock plopped completely into me. A spasm of pain flashed through me as his organ invaded my body. I wanted his cock too much to stop now. The pain immediately turned to pleasure as he continued to inch his stiff prick into me.

I concentrated solely on the hard shaft that was being shoved firmly into my body. He filled me with pleasure, the type of feeling that only a masculine stud can share with another man. I thanked my luck for finding suck a hunky stud to oblige me with his hard Air Guard cock.

Norm was patient but insistent as he worked his shaft into the tight depths of my butt hole. Occasionally, he would stop for a few seconds to let me grow accustomed to his massive tool. I was intent on taking him to the hilt without a whimper. I wanted to show this handsome Air Guard Tech Sergeant what us Marines were made of. I was a corporal in the Terran Colonial Guard and I was going to take it like a man. I wanted to be fucked and wasn't going to back out now, even if his butch cock ripped me apart.

With one last firm shove I felt the last half inch of his cock enter me. The bristly pubic hair covering his crotch was pressed firmly against the hard globes of my ass cheeks.

Norm leaned forward pressing his sweaty chest firmly against the back of my up-raised legs. Looking through my legs I could see Norm's chest, covered with a thick pelt of black hair. I loved the sight of Norm's hairy chest and abdomen where the hair thinned out a bit. But what I really liked looking at was sight of Norm's massive cock sticking out his groin area, I could see the base of the hairy cock that was sticking so far up my butt. What a fucking hot sight, good-looking stud with his cock deep in me.

My own cock was throbbing, leaking man juice all over my stomach.

"Nice ass, Corp. Hot and tight like a G.I. should be," Norm complimented.

I could feel drops of perspiration drip from Norm's hairy chest onto me. I could sense his need and urgency, but he held his cock still, rocking his hip gently side-to-side, letting me relax and grow accustomed to his length and girth.

"Hot and tight, good fucking G.I. asshole!" Norm panted. "Your butt was made to be plowed by this cock."

"Fuck me, stud!" I ordered through clenched teeth. "Show me what kind of fuckers you Air Guard boys really are."

Norm complied immediately, pulling his throbbing shaft quickly out of my ass, only to shove it firmly and manly back into me. He handled his cock like a real man, sure and certain of his fuck movement. Careful, but knowing exactly what both of us wanted. Norm began to pump me with long, slow strokes. Taking his time, he made gentle love to me, fucking me long and hard. "Tight ass," he kept saying over and over with appreciation.

"Give it to me guy, let me have that prick!" I panted.

Norm started to pick up the temp until he was ramming his cock in and out of my asshole with fury. I could feel his hairy balls slap against my own nuts on his savage down strokes.

Norm pumped his cock into me for all he was worth. And I fucking loved

his cock up my asshole. He leaned forward and kissed me with a wet, open-mouthed panting kiss. I am sure he kissed me to keep himself from yelling out with his animal passion. Although we were the only ones on the C-130, we didn't want our fucking to attract anyone's attention.

Norm gripped my shoulders and held me tightly against his husky body. Thrust after savage thrust, he pumped his hard cock deep into my guts, only to pull out a few seconds later on his up stroke. God this boy could fuck. He was built to fuck ass.

"Oh, fuck, Corp!" he yelled at last, "I'm gonna shoot my load! I'm gonna cum in your fucking asshole."

I bucked my groaning hard-on against his sweaty body. "Unload your cum in me guy, shoot that wad into me, I want your fucking load!"

Norm began to buck uncontrollably as the hot spurts of man-juice erupted from his hard cock. "Here it come, Corp—I'm cumming in your asshole...take my load stud!" Norm went wild as his man juice pumped deep inside me, white washing my bowels with his sticky cream. Every man comes differently; Norm was one of those men who went out of control when he comes. He moaned and thrashed above me, lost in his orgasm. Spasm after spasm of lust swept through his masculine body as he pumped me full of his cum. Norm's thrusts came fast and furious as he shot his load. Once or twice I thought that he was going to pull out of me completely, buy he held me tightly across the shoulders as he spent his load.

His last few thrusts clipped my prostate gland just right and brought on my own orgasm. I found myself tensing up as my own load of sperm erupted from my throbbing cock. My asshole clenched tightly around the shaft of hard cock embedded within me.

Norm moaned louder as he cock was gripped tightly by my asshole. "That's good fucking ass! Fucking tight!" he moaned. "Fucking tight and hot."

His orgasm and mine finally subsided, our fury spent in the gut-wrenching experience of cumming.

Norm relaxed his grip on my shoulders. His hairy chest was wet and slippery against me. "God, I love your ass, Corporal! Your ass was built to take a hard cock."

I leaned back on the bench seat and just enjoyed the feel and smell of this Air Guard stud's body. The shuttle reeked of sex, it smelled like male lust, and it was good.

Later when Norm pulled out of me, I was a bit sorry that it was over.

Chapter Eight

"Another round of drills, another round of replacements."

Fred and Mikael were chuckling to themselves.

I watched the shuttle drop out of the low-lying clouds and swoop over the spaceport.

"Hoping to see a familiar face?"

I looked at Fred. "Maybe." I doubted Brad would be coming back though. Sandhurst was heating up and his unit were now pulling combat duty. "Just hoping for something interesting to happen."

"Tired of guarding cargo crates?"

"Fucking right I am." *Four runs in five weeks. Boring as hell. Especially since Norm has been assigned to a different flight team.*

"Rumour says we'll be moving out soon."

"More rumours? You sucking the Major again?"

"Fuck you."

Mikael laughed loudly.

"The *Vindication* is taking on supplies. We're going to be heading out."

"What course?"

"I was talking with one of the pilots." Mikael leaned back in a chair and gave us all a grin. His reputation as a ladies' man was firmly cemented by rumours and his own outrageous stories. "In between drinks the other night, Adi told me that she's working out course jumps for Morningside."

"Morningside?"

We looked at Freddie.

He was practically shaking. "You know what's there, right?"

"No."

"Bacchus Station."

"Never heard of it."

"Fuck, Lou." Fred shook his head. "It's only the best space station for shore leave in the galaxy." He rubbed his hands together gleefully. "It's got everything. Low-grav rooms, high-grav rooms, zero-grav rooms. I've heard stories about some of the lower decks there and...well, you ain't old enough for the stories."

I just shook my head.

"So when do we jump?"

Mikael shrugged. "Adi didn't know. Soon I should think."

"Good. The sooner we leave this rock, the sooner we can have some fun."

* * *

"You seen the 'casts, Lou?'

"Not recently." I sauntered across the room towards the monitor. "You find something worth watching then?"

"Local news mostly." Mikael tapped the volume controls.

"*Carol Smythe, reporting to you live from New Providence.*" She was a buxom red-head with her hair pulled back in a severe braided hairstyle. "*'m here onboard the carrier,* C.G.. Indomitable. *We're part of the Seventh Fleet, and the first waves of reinforcements being dispatched to liberate the colonists of New Providence.*"

"Those braids look painful."

"It looks dyed."

"Quiet." Mikael shushed us. "I think I'm in love." He was staring at the reporter's image with rapt attention.

"I thought he was hot for the pilot?"

"So did I."

"Maybe *she's* hot for the reporter."

"Shut the fuck up!"

"*We've jumped into the system near the fifth planet and assumed battle formation. The Bridge has been placed off-limits to media, due to security restrictions.*

"We have already intercepted several distress calls from the planet. The people there are suffering at the hands of the rebels. Desperate voices are telling of cities destroyed, of infrastructure bombed into oblivion. People are begging for rescue and salvation."

"Bastards."

"We'll show 'em."

"Fucking right."

"Although the fleet's precise battle plans remain confidential, it's no secret that the Seven Fourteen Squadron will be making an attack run towards New Providence in advance of landing parties.

"I can hear the alert klaxon going off now. We have incoming ships and—"

The image dissolved into static. *<Uplink terminated at source>* flashed across the monitor and then it went black.

Mikael leaned back in his chair. "Fuck."

"We're no where near New Providence," I pointed out. "How'd we get that signal?"

"Some freighter jumped in a few hours ago and began transmitting. That was just the most interesting piece to be aired." Fred shrugged. "The freighter was intercepted pretty damned fast too."

"I hope she's all right."

I looked at Mikeal. "Maybe you'll be lucky and we'll be sent to reinforce New Providence. Then you can rescue her from the tedium of her career."

"Fuck you, Lou."

* * *

"Freeze!"

My chest and face hit the brick wall hard, knocking the wind out of me. My attacker, in the black uniform of an MP, pulled my hands behind me and quickly tightened the cuffs around my wrists.

"Fuck, man!" I yelled as he closed them too tight for comfort, yanking at me to get me towards his squad car. His strength was awesome as he read me my rights, and I wondered if my being distracted by his hot body would get me out because I wasn't hearing my rights. Hell, he might hurt me if I continued to resist as I had been doing.

He pushed me into the back seat of the car, bumping my head against the top of the doorframe. On purpose, I thought. He closed the door, and I looked around, noting the lack of handles on the inside of the door, and the sturdy looking cage fence that divided me from where he now sat.

He spoke into the car's radio, announcing that he'd caught me. His partner, another MP, had gone around the other side of the building, and was now returning. "So, Rob, you got the little bastard," he said as he looked at me through the grate.

"Yeah, Mitch!" he said. "The son of a bitch put up a fight too! You know that adds resisting arrest to your charges, don't you?" He hit the grate with all of that magnificent strength, startling me.

"Damned punk!" the other MP said as they got going. The streets of New Wessex were dirty and filled with people far worse than me, but I had gotten caught, hadn't I? Rob kept looking back at me through the rear view mirror, and I couldn't help but taunt him a bit. Smiling and even blowing him a kiss or two every time he looked. Hell, risk-taking was my nature and it led me into the Colonial Guard and it's what got me into trouble tonight.

I'd left the compound for some *real* shore leave. I needed sex badly. So badly it hurt. I was willing to fuck anyone anywhere anytime, and tonight had been the turn of a frisky young man I met at a local gay bar. I'm partial to young men and this guy had gotten me as hard as a fucking rock the instant I spotted him.

Anyway, I met this young stud at the bar, and it clicked almost immediately. He had a blond crew cut, blue eyes, chiselled body that was not beefy, perpetually wet lips that gave his smile a hot & nasty appeal that I simply could not resist. The snag in all this was his friends. He was stuck to them like glue. He looked at me, smiling that evil smile, shifting his weight around every once in a while so as to offer me a good view of that beautiful round ass that made a joke of his somewhat baggy jeans. I couldn't catch much of a glance at his crotch, but it was obviously ample. The smiles and movements continued for over two hours, and I was loving it. The rest of the bar might as well not have existed at all. Finally, he was alone. *Would it only be for a minute?* I couldn't wait to see. I moved in, introducing myself in as overtly sexual a way as I could without the use of profanity.

"I'm Greg," he said, smiling that smile again. He recoiled just a bit as I touched his face, but allowed it. His face was smooth as silk to my fingers. His lips parted slightly as my right middle finger touched his lips, and he kissed it.

"Oh, yes!" I said. "I know what you want."

Grabbing his hand in mine, I led him outside and around the corner into the alleyway that separated the buildings housing the bar and deli. He didn't say a word. I spotted the dumpster and headed for the far side. With any luck there would already be someone there and this could turn into a real party. That was not the case, however.

We reached the other side of the dumpster, and not being one to waste any of our precious time, I put my hand at the back of his neck and pulled him in for a kiss. My hair fell over my face, providing a bit of a tickle to our faces that made him laugh. I kissed him again for having such a sweet laugh, and he put his hands to my chest, feeling the muscles and being impressed by what he felt. I grabbed hold of his flannel shirt and yanked it open. He looked down at what I'd done and then at me.

"I'll buy you another," I told him as he gave me the smile again and put his hand on my crotch to feel what he was in for. His wet lips opened as he felt it. Pounding strongly with its own pulse and warm with the flow of blood, even through the heavy jeans.

"Seven and a half!" I said to him, watching the look on his face change from surprise to desire.

He immediately went for the belt, undoing it in seconds. The button fly came undone so fast I didn't even notice it. He reached in, and I jumped as I felt his cool hand on my cock "You're hot," he said. A simple statement that required no answer from me. Just as quickly, he knelt before me, pulling down my jeans and licking his lips. He took my foreskin in both hands, his thumbs on the inside, index fingers clamping onto it on the outside as he stretched it. He was more than happy to see it extend a good two inches from the tip of my cock, which was already engorged. He rubbed it slowly, sending sharp sensations through my body. I looked down at him once my eyes felt ready to open from the prior sensations, and was treated to the view of his tongue as it worked its way into the foreskin. "Mmmmm!" was all I could manage at the time, and his response was to make little circles on my cock head with his tongue.

A friend once told me that a blow job was a blow job. That no matter who gave it, it felt pretty much the same.

He pushed the foreskin back as far as it would go and put the head gently in his mouth. The sensation was minimal, but powerful because of that very fact. It glistened as he took it out of his mouth, wet with his spit. He then closed his lips tight, and took my dick into his mouth. His lips opened only grudgingly as he put his hands on my ass to pull me toward him. It felt like I was fucking a tight hole, I swear it did.

"Yeah!" I said a little too loudly, and began to fuck his face. Every time I pulled out, he allowed the head to leave his mouth only to have it force its way back in through his pursed lips. I was in heaven. I fucked and fucked his beautiful face until I almost came, but I wasn't about to let it end there. I pulled out of his mouth and turned around, offering him my ass. He offered no objection and went right in, burying his face between my well developed glutes. Within seconds, my ass was wet with his spittle. His tongue was probing deeply, wanting to go where it could not. I bent my knees and lowered myself, giving him better access to my hole. I could see between my own legs that his hard cock was sticking out of the open zipper, large as my own his right hand stroking it furiously as the left helped him with his ass licking.

I reached down to remove my jeans, difficult without removing my shoes, but, in this instance, doable. Once they were off, I was no longer constrained, and I would have what I wanted. I turned suddenly.

I grabbed Greg under the arms and lifted him up to meet my lips. I kissed him hard, leaving no doubt as to the state of my horniness. Turned him around and finished removing his shirt. I felt him shiver as I put my mouth to the back of his neck and began licking downward, following his spine to the waiting prize. I pulled down his jeans and finally, his ass stared me in the face, and my mouth watered. Like a hungry animal, I tore into it. Licking it, probing it with my tongue, being overwhelmed by the sweet smell of him while he moaned in pleasure. My face was surely glistening with my own spit and sweat, and I could feel him loosening up. I touched the hole with a couple of finger, and felt him move to accept them. Slowly I pushed both fingers into him, stopping every so often as I felt him tense up. I pulled back and as he relaxed forged ahead. I reached under him with my other hand, taking hold of his lovely cut cock and stroking it gently. I twisted, turned and bent my fingers inside him as he began to moan. "Yeah! You want it!" I said. "Are you ready?"

"Do it!"

I stood and pulled him up against me. I leaned against the wall behind me, his neck just a little below the level of my own. I kissed it. Bit it. I reached down and positioned myself for entry. He sighed his approval. I reached around him, hugging him tight, rubbing my hands along his sculptured chest and abs. I pushed to the sound of his gasp, but I didn't, couldn't stop.

"Oh!" he said as his back arched and his head fell back against my shoulder. Inch by inch I penetrated him until I felt his tailbone up against my pubes. I reached up with a hand, and turned his pretty face toward me. I buried my tongue in his mouth just as my cock was buried in his hot hole and reached for his cock. His breath was heavy as I fucked him, kissed him, jerked him off. His body was alive with subtle movements, and mine moved in its rhythm. In and out I went, relishing the sensations I felt. Feeling alive and loving it. He began to moan loudly, and I increased my pumping action, both as I fucked him and as I stroked his cock. He came with a bang, blowing his wad like I'd never seen before. It flew everywhere, shooting out of him like a bullet from a gun. I fucked him harder and harder, and I could feel that he was getting hard again. I put my hand to his face, pulling it toward me, turning it. I put my lips to his mouth and pushed my tongue into his mouth. I used my other hand to pull him tight, burying cock deep inside him as the cum flew. "Oh fucking yes!" I yelled into his mouth, feeling my whole body become week, as if all of my energy had flown with the cum that now flew deep into him. I continued to kiss him, my body pumping what seemed an eternal amount of cum into him. It stopped, and both of our bodies relaxed, my cock was becoming soft inside him, providing yet another sensation I cannot accurately describe. We stayed that way for several minutes, kissing each other wildly.

Greg pulled away, reluctantly giving up the kisses I offered. He pulled on his pants and his now-buttonless shirt, and I did the same. As he attempted to tuck in his shirt, I finished with my own clothing, and knelt back down before him. His cock was still hard after rising that second time, and I took it in my mouth. It felt so good, the slight taste of cum, that undeniably masculine smell. I sucked him hard, furiously. He moaned loudly. I gave him no mixed signals here. I wanted his cum wanted it bad. It didn't take long, however, before my mouth was filled with his delicious cum. He seemed to collapse in front of me, falling to his knees. I kissed him, and gave it all back to him. We kissed and swirled the cum in each others' mouths until it had all vanished.

We stood, he zipped his fly, I wiped a little cum off my face with a finger and put it delicately in my mouth. Suddenly there was panic.

"Hey!" we heard someone yell,

"Shit! Cops!"

A military policeman was standing there, flashlight in hand and pointed directly at us.

Greg and I thought alike, and ran in the opposite direction. Somewhere down the alley I lost him, he'd gone toward the right, I toward the left where the alley met up with a third building and split in two. I ran like a cheetah, and heard the MP yelling at me to stop as he ran behind me. Suddenly it was over, the tallest fucking fence you ever saw stood between me and the street beyond.

I tried climbing it anyway, but the MP grabbed hold of my belt and pulled me back down. He slammed me against the wall and cuffed me, reading me my rights. This, of course, is where we started.

He made several turns along the way, and as I thought of the how of all this, I'd lost track of where we were going. The second MP looked back at me every once in a while, a look of utter disdain on his otherwise pretty face.

We pulled up to an old, and apparently abandoned building. "Oh shit," I said quietly. These two were going to beat the shit out of me or something. My heart began to beat hard in panic. I began to babble as they pulled me from the car. "Hey, guys!" I pleaded. "Come on. Don't do this. Please!" I continued to babble as they pushed me into the building.

This was a very old building indeed, and great parts of the walls were missing, giving just enough cover in the darkness of night, but easy enough access for entry or escape. They continued to push me inward, leading me into a hallway somewhere in the heart of the building. The MP carried something in his hand, and he set it on one of the steps that lead to a mostly nonexistent second floor. He pushed me up against the wall, and removing my cuffs, tied me to a leather strap that was somehow attached to the wall. The strap, quite strong I assure you, held my waist with smaller straps on the side where he now placed my hands to hold them in place. I was scared out of my mind, and closed my eyes, expecting the first blow.

I was shocked when I felt hands on my crotch, two pairs in fact!

I opened my eyes to Rob's stare. He'd knelt down before me, and slowly massaged my bulge. "Nice," he commented.

The military policeman stood in front of me. "You do realize that lewd behaviour is punishable with a substantial fine...and probably jail time," he asked.

"We were—" I began.

"Shut it. There's no excuse for breaking the law, scum-ball."

Arrogant twat, I thought.

"The current penalty in this area is one year forced labour," the cop went on, a sadistic tone in his voice.

"How do you feel about having to pay that?"

I smiled, sweetly. "I'd prefer not to, obviously," I said.

The policeman grinned menacingly. "I'll bet you wouldn't," he said, scratching his ear with his pencil. "I suppose we can always give you an oral warning."

"Don't you mean a *verbal* warning?" I asked, puzzled.

"I know what I mean," Rob muttered, removing his flat police cap. As if it was some kind of signal the other cop stepped into my view. "Need any help, Rob?" he asked? He wasn't wearing his peaked cap either, but unlike the first officer this one was blonde and fresh-faced, much younger than his dark partner.

The cop called Rob shook his head. "I think our friend's going to be co-operative, aren't you, son?" he said, an evil leer on his face.

Seeing as I was tied up, I began to feel uneasy. "Sure. I'll do whatever you say. Am I under arrest then?" I asked.

The two cops smiled and exchanged a knowing look. "Not if you play ball," the dark one grinned. He must have been in his early thirties, a good ten years older than his blonde pal.

I wasn't sure if I was doing the right thing by "playing ball", but what choice did I have?

"Now what shall we do first?" Rob asked.

"I know," Mitch replied with a leer. "Why doesn't our pal here give us a show? A strip show!"

I shook my head. "Wait a fucking minute! I'm not doing a strip for nobody!"

Rob's eyes narrowed. "Not even if it means saving your skin from an assault charge?"

"Assault?" I gasped. "What bloody assault?"

"Don't you remember how you tried to kick the shit out of me when I grabbed you in the alley? Mitch here remembers because he had to help me subdue you. That's how you got your bruises."

"I don't have any bruises."

Mitch smiled. "It can be arranged."

"So how about it?" his partner asked. "Why not take your clothes off like a good 'un, and then we can let you go on your way without any further hassle."

Reluctantly, I had to agree and Rob untied me. With my eyes fixed firmly on the floor, I took off my shoes and socks, tucking the socks neatly inside the shoes and then laying the shoes to one side.

"Picky little snot, aren't you?"

I shot Mitch a nasty look. Feeling extremely self-conscious, I unbuttoned my shirt slowly. I had a good body, and in normal circumstances I wasn't ashamed of showing it off. But under the watchful eyes of the two policemen, I felt shy.

"That's it. Don't be shy." Rob was burning into rubbing his left hand between his legs as he spoke.

I unzipped my jeans and pushed them down to my ankles. Kicking them off, I slipped my briefs down as well and stood there, naked.

"Now that's better, isn't it?" Rob asked, as though I were a child. "Just like you were in the alley." He chuckled. "But we wouldn't want you to feel like the odd one out, would we, Mitch?"

The blond shook his head. "No way," he answered, unzipping his dark blue trousers.

As I watched the young policeman took off his trousers and removed his underpants. His cock was large, although quite slim, uncircumcised and fully erect. The bulbous head was wet and shiny, and the bed of pubic curls between his legs was surprisingly fair.

"I hope you like sucking cock," Rob said.

"Yes," I replied. I could feel my own prick beginning to throb. I was about to be sexually assaulted and I was getting a hard-on!

Rob stepped out of his trousers and briefs. He stood there with hairy muscular thighs and a dense bush of wiry dark curls in his crotch, from which hung his large heavy balls. His dick was circumcised and sleek, and stood out erect from his groin, arching slightly to the right...perhaps as a result of too much jerking off as a kid. "Okay, son," he said holding his cock by the shaft and stroking it. "Time for a bit of cock-sucking, don't you think, Mitch?"

The younger cop, who was standing next to Rob and slowly stroking his own erection, gave a big stupid grin and lowered his head to his pal's lap. I watched totally fascinated as Mitch took Rob's cock in his mouth without hesitation, sliding his sensuous full lips up and down the shaft as Rob stroked the young guy's short blond locks.

I was unable to tear my eyes from the blatant display in front of me, and even as I watched I became aware that I was playing with myself. I was getting as horny as the two policemen obviously were, the sight of the two half-naked cops engaging in oral sex making my cock tingle with excitement.

Rob touched Mitch's neck, easing his head up so that just the swollen pink cock-head was still between the guy's lips. Mitch ran his tongue around the rim of the cock-head, tracing the line of the faint white circumcision scar. "Now I think it's time he earned his freedom," Rob said, pulling Mitch's head up and away from his crotch. Rob motioned to me.

I dropped to me knees on the floor in front of him. I took hold of Rob's penis, now wet with both Mitch's saliva and the first smears of pre-cum, and, lowering my head, I gobbled the cock in one swoop, letting Rob thrust it deep into my throat. I could taste the copper's semen, salty and slightly bitter, and with my face buried in Rob's pubic hair I could smell the heady, overpowering scent of muskiness. I drew my mouth back and forth along the thick shaft, taking the cock so deep I almost gagged before drawing it out until just the very tip was still between my lips. I repeated this for a while, loving the feel of another man's hard prick in my mouth, the soft gentle moaning which was coming from Rob seeming like music to my ears and spurring him on.

I had his eyes closed, and in the cool darkness of the room, I felt the warmth of a hand between my legs and knew it must be Mitch. I was being manoeuvred so that the lower half of my body was twisted sideways, my bare ass on the floor and my legs outstretched. A moment later I felt the exquisite wet sensation of Mitch's mouth between my legs. The young cop was licking the inside of my thighs, working up to my balls. He closed off his mind, so powerful was the urge to shoot my load instantly, and concentrated on sucking Rob's hot throbbing manhood.

I ran my tongue along the thick vein on the underside of Rob's cock, starting at the root and working up to the bulbous dick-head. I squeezed the head gently so that the small piss-hole at the tip opened, and, using my eager tongue, I licked at the semen which was seeping out.

I stopped for a moment, gasping as he felt Mitch take my prick into his mouth. The cop was obviously an expert when it came to giving a blow-job, and I was so aroused by the unexpected 'session' that I was very close to my climax.

So, apparently, was Rob. His hips gyrated slightly as I sucked at his cock, and his scrotum seemed tight and full. Suddenly he grabbed my hair, yanked my head back so that his cock slipped out of my mouth, and hunched over me. He grabbed his cock and began stroking it furiously. A gob of thick white cum spurted powerfully from the cop's dick, splattering in my face and running down the bridge of my nose and cheeks. More and more spunk shot forth, until I was drenched in the warm milky juice.

When he'd finished, Rob released the fistful of hair he had and stepped away. He motioned to Mitch, who was merrily chomping on my fat rod, and the young cop stopped, knelt before me and proceeded to lick the dripping cum from my face.

I took hold of Mitch's prick and jerked it even as the cop licked me clean. As a last gesture, Mitch licked the last of the cum from my chin, then slipped his tongue into my mouth and kissed me. I tasted Rob's cum in my mouth as our tongues intertwined.

Encouraged by Rob, Mitch and I assumed a sixty-nine position, I on my back on the floor with Mitch above me. Mitch had my cock in his mouth in an instant, sucking eagerly on the sticky organ. I took the cop's erection between my lips, repeating the actions that had brought Rob off so quickly.

As I sucked Mitch off, I reached up to caress Mitch's buttocks. From my horizontal position, I could see that Rob was fingering Mitch's ass, and I knew that cock-sucking and good anal stimulation together are guaranteed to have a guy coming in no time.

Mitch was close, very close to shooting his load, but then so was I! I could see the way the cop's bodily instincts had taken over his gyrations. He was moving rhythmically, but without being aware of it, and as he swayed left and right I felt his shaft twitch and rise, growing even harder if it was at all possible. Mitch ejaculated. He was thrusting and pushing, causing his cock to plunge deeper down my throat. I gagged, but Mitch never let up. Spunk shot from Mitch's penis and I felt my mouth fill with cum. I swallowed it, gulping down the juice quickly in an effort to stem the tide which was spurting down my throat. At the same time I felt his own climax building, and I shot my own load, the young blond cop drinking up the tasty warm fluid.

We sucked each other dry, Mitch's hot cock growing limp in my mouth and Mitch releasing my dick from his. Then we sagged back, exhausted by the sheer force of the passion we'd just indulged in.

The two cops dressed quickly and in complete silence, buttoning up their tunics as though nothing had happened.

"Come on, get dressed," Rob finally said. "Unless you want to come back to the station house with us."

"No thanks." I scrambled for my clothing and dressed faster than I ever had in my life before.

Rob gestured to the doorway. "Get lost."

Chapter Nine

The *Vindication* jumped and headed towards Elysia.

The squad had gathered together in the mess hall. We just congregated there, without any real plans to do so, and we massed around a cluster of tables at the back of the room.

Mikael was grinning when he brought his mug of coffee to join us. "No doubt even you shit-heads have already got this figured out, but we finally got us a combat mission."

"No shit."

The mess hall was quiet.

"We're going to have some ground action."

"Probably."

"We're gonna see some serious action."

"Fucking A."

"What's the target?"

"Civie government trying to revolt. We'll just drop in and they'll probably fold."

I smiled. "Just like that."

"Hey, we know our history. You think they don't?"

The Company did have a history. "Hearing that the *Truculent* are heading towards you should a sobering effect on the rebels." I shrugged. "Or encourage them to blow up the ship before we reach orbit."

"If we get hit, we get hit." Fred shrugged and then took a drink of his coffee. "We can't do shit about it."

Very true. We were just marines—passengers—onboard the frigate.

"What about Morningside?"

All eyes shifted towards Mikael.

"Yeah, what about Bacchus?"

"I think we're still stopping there. Adi didn't say anything about Elysia."

"Plans change." I sipped my coffee. "The brass don't care if we get our rocks off before dying."

"We might be stopping near Morningside though. The *Vindication* can't be the only ship going in. We must be meeting up with a task force."

"You hope so."

"I heard the Thirty-Second Platoon is practising urban assault sims."

"Lucky them."

* * *

I wasn't actually looking for any tight, hard marine butt at that particular moment. When you're deployed for months on an extended patrol with seven hundred other marines and a few hundred dick-hungry sailors, checking out ass in the shower is the last thing you should do. I got really good at going through the day with blinders on, ignoring the packages in the weight room, the dicks swinging and slapping hard marine thighs in berthing, the ball bags hanging heavy and low. A lot of other guys on the ship might have wanted the same things I did, but there were also others around who claim they didn't want a thick dick up their butts. They probably did, of course, but would eat nails before they'd admit how they really felt.

Even in my straight-arrow mode, there was no way I could let Rick's bouncy bubble butt slide past with a casual glance. Nearly every active duty marine has a good ass. But, even by marine standards, Rick's butt was epic. He didn't have a hint of slack and his great, hard muscled butt jutted out proudly from his hips. It

was hairless and tanned and had the rich, soft transient glow of youth.

Rick was nineteen, pretty fresh from the Academy with a handful of missions under his belt. His hard body was like steel bands tightly coiled within tender skin. He was all rippling muscle so soft to the touch that you would almost rather admire him than fuck him.

Almost.

That day, I lost control of myself. He was turned away from the door so I didn't think he'd notice. My eyes shamelessly took in his hard flesh until he turned quickly around and caught me looking at him. I tried to cover with something about looking for a towel I'd left behind, but I blushed and stammered and I did everything but sink open-mouthed to my knees.

After that, I was smart enough to steer clear of him for a while and I might have been okay if I'd scored ashore in Bacchaus Station. Our last night in, though, I struck out again for a perfect record: zero for four.

Getting drunk was a mistake. For one thing, it didn't help ease any of my frustration. For another, it made me even hornier—if that were possible. By the time I got back to the *Vindication*, I was in sad shape and sick. My idea—to the point I was thinking clearly enough that night even to have an idea—was to shower and fall into my rack to sleep off my desire and frustration along with my drunken state. Sure enough, though, fate decided something else. Rick stood bare-assed, flexing his muscles and admiring himself in the shower when I got there. And we were alone!

Fuck it, I thought to myself. I tore off my Tee-shirt and shorts and tossed them into the trash, threw my towel to the deck and slipped into the shower where Rick was smearing foamy white suds across his beautiful bare backside. He started to look around, but I wasn't in the mood for a fucking conversation. I lay my left hand across his strong, tanned shoulders and pushed his face to the wall of the shower. With my other hand, I soaped the crack in his butt.

I rubbed the slick suds deep between his massive muscles, spreading his cheeks wide as the hot water coursed down his back and splashed off his ass onto my legs. His butt instinctively began to grind against my hand, softly at first and then as loudly as he dared, he let moans and whimpers of pleasure ooze up from his lips. His butt, soft, hairless and strong, wriggled in my hand until, almost as though by accident, my fuck finger slipped into the pucker that bounded his virtue—and my need.

I attacked his wet neck and shoulders with my mouth. His body was writhing against the shower wall, so my restraining hand was free to slide across his bootcamp-cut hair and down across his massive hairless chest. I tweaked his hard, passion tipped tits, but I didn't finger fuck his ass. I didn't have to. He was grinding and thrusting and gyrating so much that his butthole wriggled up my fuck finger on its own. When he cried out and I knew Rick had been longing to have me inside him as much as I'd needed to be there, I suddenly felt not only sober, but almost liberated. Peace was just a soapy butt-fuck away.

I took my time with him. I hadn't been inside another man in three months, but some deep, ancient urging slowed my pace and made me savour the texture of his slick ass chute along my finger, the stubble of his hair against my palm, the thrill of his shoulder against my lips and the deep moans of pleasure that he emitted.

My chest was against his back and I felt his slick, naked flesh slide against my fur-covered skin. For the first time, my attention turned from his ass to his youthful face. In many ways, he was an Alexander—hard and lean and fit for battle, yet blessed with a pug nose and green eyes and enough freckles to decorate a tribe of leprechauns. And Rick's body was the beauty of man incarnate—the best of the young, the glory of a hunk in his prime, and, as he soon proved, the perfection of a stud skilled beyond his years.

I wasn't about to stand behind him all night with his butt wrapped around my finger. I had something much meatier in mind. My thick nine inches slid between his soapy ass cheeks and eased against his wrinkled hole. His hole kissed my cock-head, begging me to hurry, and as my tongue darted into his ear, his body convulsed against me, driving his tight manhole up my throbbing crankshaft. He slipped over my purple, passion-pulsing knob in one swift stroke and lingered for a brief moment. Then, a second seizure even more violent than the first sent him lunging up my shaft until all nine inches of my joint were embedded inside his guts.

I lay quietly inside him for a moment. Then, I worked my stiff pubes against his tight Marine butt and ground into him, twisting my cock inside his fuck tunnel, shoving my hard dickhead into the nether regions of his body. His rapid, frenzied pants grew even more erratic as I began a long, slow withdrawal—pulling about eight of my thick nine inches from him. Only my trigger-ridge kept his ass hooked, but lust had swollen me wide and I was his for the duration.

When I fucked back into him, my hips jolted with a thwack into his hard jock ass and almost before that sound could ricochet off the shower walls, I was leaving him again, stroking up and slamming down like a piston in a runaway engine. I felt his slick flesh sliding along my cock rail like a fucking express to ecstasy. Our bodies rammed against each other. I grasped him from the front and pulled him even farther up my prick and pounded him harder and faster. Delirious need gripped us both and drove us frantically onward.

Every time my hips bashed against Rick's classic ass, every time my cock skewered into him, he let out a grunt of satisfaction. We were lost in ecstasy, and I don't know how long we rammed and fucked. Eventually, I heard a cry that grew louder until I realized it was my own. Almost at once, white-hot pulses coursed up through my cum-chute and out through the huge nozzle I had parked deep inside Rick's ass.

Now that Rick had a taste of dick, he was ready for more. Even before I was completely free of his hole, he was trying to spin me around to use me as he wanted. He sank to his knees and buried his pug nose up my butt. I'd never been much into rimming, but, then, I'd never felt Rick's talented tongue up my butt. The bastard wasn't about to give me a chance to catch my breath. That nose slid along the hairy crack of my ass like Patton through Germany.

When it hit home, his tongue took over and drilled deep while that innocent little pug nose shuddered from side to side to keep my well muscled ass from closing in.

Rick wasn't just a tongue fucker; he was an artist. The tip of his tongue attacked my fuck hole, dancing around the rim, gliding between the folds of my twitching pucker and pounding into the pit. Every flick and stroke and slice of his tongue tip jolted me to the core and slipped me deeper into my lust-struck trance. I could have stood there with my legs apart, that boyish face up by butt forever.

Petting the back of his head as though he were a puppy, I remember being surprised at how soft Rick's hair was. It was more like a cat's than a man's. But, since he was going to be my space pussy for the next few months, I guess that was appropriate. Just then, I was trying not to moan too loudly. The last thing I needed at that moment was a skulk of marines to slink in to join the action. I wanted Rick's tongue all to myself and, fortunately, Rick didn't seem to mind.

He moved around and shoved the biggest, thickest dick I'd ever seen into my face. All I could do was gape at it in admiration and then it was in my throat. I managed to pull him out enough to allow my tongue to do justice to the huge, sloppy foreskin that dangled from the front of the gorgeous dick. My tongue slid between the loose flesh and the silky-smooth man meat that lay hidden below. I found his cum-slit lost under the secret folds of his manhood and began to slither in and out of his gash. I slurped greedily with shameless abandonment.

Rick's luscious knob slid back to make a home in the tight, tender tissues of my throat as his hips began slamming his meat farther and deeper into my face. I reached round to grab the butt I'd just fucked, but this time I was on the receiving end of the dick-and loving every face-slapping minute.

Young Rick liked ramming his dork down my gullet for a while. His moans and grunts and cocky leers of pleasure showed well enough that he thought he was in charge. From there, though, he took about ten seconds to discover that tight as my throat was, I had another hole that would be even more fun. I suppose the studly thing to do would have been for me to deprive him, but turn about is fair play. He had his dick set on a good, solid butt-fuck, so I got to my feet, turned round and spread my ass.

I was ready for him to hurt. Any dick that size would have to, I thought. For the first six or eight seconds, it did. Quickly, however, the pain turned to pleasure. Something about the way I was turned on changed everything. Maybe it was the way Rick was playing with my tits and the way his teeth had locked themselves into the back of my neck. Maybe it was the delicious wickedness of fucking a brother Marine in the shower of a Navy frigate. Whatever it was, before his throbbing member was shaft-deep up my tight, slutty fuck-hole, I was one very happy man. Every sensation that should have been agony turned to ecstasy and showed me how much fun being on the other end of the stick could be.

Rick grew all butch and used me like his personal whore—and I loved it! Within a few minutes, his method of fucking had given me an anal orgasm—the first of many that night. Once I'd turned him on, there wasn't any stopping the guy and he fucked my butt until I thought we were both goners. By the time I felt his pearly cum up my ass, I was ready to fuck him. We kept at it, fucking and loving and teaching each other the ways of real male love until we were both exhausted and reveille brought more men into the head. They gave us sly looks as we limped out to our racks, but by then, neither of us much gave a fuck. We were just too fucking tired.

Chapter Ten

I drew my combat armour. Ferro-ceramic vest and helmet. Hot and sweaty to wear, even with the cooling Kevlar jumpsuit underneath it. But it would help keep me alive on the battlefields, so it was worth wearing.

Too bad no one looked good in one.

Rick walked past, already suited up. He gave me a nod.

I nodded back. *Can't even see his ass in that suit.* I shook my head. *Focus on the mission. No point in getting killed over his cock.*

The other marines finished suiting up and we checked each other's armour just like we did in practice drills.

"*Stand by for the final jump.*"

This was the part I hated. Waiting for the ship to plunge through hyperwarp and emerge into orbit of whatever our target world was. In this case, Elysia.

The ship lurched slightly as we ended the jump.

The light panels flickered and then returned to normal intensity.

"*Jump completed,*" a voice echoed over the intercom. "*Orbital insertion completed.*" There was a brief pause. "*Launch landers.*"

"Fucking A!" Fred cried out as the landing craft burned towards the surface. "We came out right on top of them!"

"So now we drop groundward."

"It's not the drop that will kill you," Mikael reminded us in a soft voice. "It's that sudden stop at the end."

I checked my seat restraints.

The shuttle bucked as it entered the atmosphere.

* * *

Bullets spranged past my helmet.

"Snipers!" someone shouted.

By the time I turned around, half a dozen marines had pinpointed the source of enemy fire and *neutralized* it. A nice clean euphemism for turning a living person into ground meat.

"Welcome to fucking Cotswald." Fred kicked at a sign post. "A hundred lightyears from home and it looks just like that shit-pile."

"Welcome to the Marines. See the galaxy, meet new people...and kill them." Mikael stepped around crater.

I studied the area. It looked peaceful...too peaceful really because the spaceport was quiet. *Nothing launching. Nothing landing. Just peace and quiet and a life or death war raging just out of our sight.*

The bulk of the city's buildings rose in the distance. Columns of smoke rose from a dozen locations between the block skyscrapers.

Earl was holding a com-set to his head. "Perimeter sweep completed, Major. The spaceport is secured."

Mostly, I amended.

"Limited sniper action. It should be safe to bring in the rest of the unit." Earl's eyes scanned the horizon. "Resistance is minimal."

"No one around here to shoot," Freddie muttered. "What kind of rebellion is this?"

"A small one."

A fresh column of smoke began to rise from beyond the buildings.

"New orders, Marines!" Earl gestured, one hand still holding the radio. "We're supposed to hook up with the Thirty-Second and execute a sweep along the river. Lieutenant Chang is reporting contact with enemy forces."

Mikael smiled. "Finally, some decent action."

Earl groaned and shook his head. "You ain't served with those screw-ups yet."

I frowned at that.

* * *

"I'm glad I could die for my world," moaned Lieutenant Chang.

Now Corporal Mallen, the squad's medic became as frustrated as he was furious. "Jesus Christ on a stick, Ell-tee! That's the fifth goddamn time you've said that in the last five goddamn minutes! And you're not even hit, goddamn it!"

Chang smiled gently. "I know you're just talking me down, Jim, but I can't feel my legs."

"That's because Jackson is lying on them! Goddamn it, sir, if you don't get up and start leading the men, I'll shoot you myself!"

"There's a lot more of them than we thought." I was crouched behind a fallen tree trunk and using it for cover. Bullets smacked into the wood with dull thunks as I ducked. "Shit!"

Rick was hunkered down somewhere behind me with the radio. "We blundered into an ambush! We need evac. Do you copy?"

Private Danny Varney, the squad's heavy machine gunner—who was six foot five and built like a three hundred pound brick wall—bellowed between bursts. "Get some! Get some, you fuckers! Yeah! You like that, don't you? Fucking scum!"

I dove behind a fallen tree and squeezed off a round. *No targets, so no point in wasting ammo on auto-fire.*

"What a cock-up!" Mikael had his own bit of cover which he hugged as bullets whined overhead. "Where'd the rebels get this much firepower?"

"Must be part of the rogue militia."

A stray round grazed Varney in the shoulder.

"Motherf—remorseless, treacherous, lecherous, kindless villain!" Varney was known to become poetic when he was hit, despite of his gung-ho wildman nature. He had been sent to a C.G.. shrink once, after he was found weeping at the remains of his squad, reciting verses of Shakespeare's Hamlet. He had managed to exterminate an entire rebel company after an ambush caught the rest of his squad in a deadly hail of fire. Luckily for Varney, he had been just fifty metres behind the rest of his squadmates, tying his boot laces of all things, when the rebels sprung their trap. The psychiatrist had concluded it was Varney's way of dealing with stress and shipped him back to his outfit. After all, despite being prone to pissing off the rest of the squad with his ramblings, he was a fine, outstanding killing machine.

Now he stood up, stabilized his *Enfield M-90* and started ripping off long bursts with the light machine gun. "Or to take arms against a sea of troubles!" *Rat-tat-tat-tat-tat-tat* "And by opposing end them? To die, to sleep—no more!" *Rat-tat-tat-tat-tat-tat-tat-tat* "And by a sleep to say we end!" *rat-tat-tat rat-tat* "The heartache and the thousand!" *rat-tat-tat-tat-tat-tat*

"Lieutentant!" screamed Mallen. "We have to do something!"

Lieutenant Chang suddenly snapped out of it and jumped to his feet, a look of amazement on his face. He hopped around and stared at his legs. "It's a miracle, Corporal! A miracle! I can walk!" the exhilerated lieutenant yelled, "I'll see to it that you get the bronze star!"

"I don't want a fucking bronze star, Ell-tee! I want you to do something, sir!"

"Okay, Corporal, I'll make it a silver star!"

""No, goddamn it! I don't want any fucking medals, I want you to get us the goddamn hell out of here!"

"You drive a hard bargain, Corporal! A silver star and a distinguished service cross!"

"Fuck, sir! We don't have time for this!" Mallen opened up with his own *Ratler* and managed to fire off a few bursts before he noticed a *potato masher* landing in the middle of the bomb crater our squad was holed up in.

"Grenade!" bellowed Freddie. He developed almost super-human speed in his reaction to the immediate threat to us, and dove for the grenade, scooped it up, and threw it back towards the rebels.

The explosion pelted us with dirt.

Rocks rained down on us and one hit Lieutenant Chang, knocking him flat on his face. "Medic! came the call from the lieutenant. "Mallen! I'm hit! I'm dying, Mal!"

"Christ, not again!" yelled the immensely frustrated medic as he scurried over to the stunned Lieutenant to attempt yet again to rouse their fatalistic leader into action.

"Mal! I told you! I knew this would be the day! I don't want you to think I'm crazy, but the rat that lives under my hooch came up to me last night and told me I would die today. I accept my fate, Mal! It's amazing, but I feel like my whole life has been leading up to this point! To give my life for my men, and..."

This was the moment Mallen hated the most about every time Chang would give one of his death speeches.

"I'm glad I could die for my world," said Chang softly.

Mallen seethed with anger. He grabbed the Lieutenant by the collar and slapped him twice. "Ell-tee! Goddamn it! You're not dying! You're not even hit!"

Chang smiled gently, as though he was talking to a child. "I know, Mal. I know."

"Sir! Goddamn it! I'm not kidding! You're not injured!"

"Mal, I've got a sharp pain in my head."

"That's from a rock!"

Just then, we all heard the soft *swoosh* of inbound hoppers.

"Ours?" Freddie asked in a soft voice.

"Better be," I answered.

The radio crackled alive. "*Mongoose Three-Two, this is Dustoff lead, do you read?*"

Mallen, excited to know he was getting out of the trouble they were in, tore the radio from Rick's hands. "Roger that Dustoff! This is Mongoose Three-Two, we copy! Get us the hell out of here!"

"*Mongoose, calm down. We don't see you, pop lemon smoke!*"

Mallen, knowing the rebels would be listening and attempting to lure the hoppers over to them, hastily tried to recall which color of smoke lemon was the code-equivalent of. He quickly grabbed a red smoke grenade and yanked the pin off. "Dustoff, this is Mongoose, confirm lemon smoke!"

"Mongoose, this is Dustoff, we see lime, you dumb bastard."

That obviously meant Mallen had remembered the code wrong. The only option left was the green smoke. He grabbed the grenade and pulled off the pin. "Dustoff, this is Mongoose, confirm lemon smoke this time!"

"Roger that, Mongoose, we confirm lemon this time. Get your codes right the next time, you dumb bastard, or I'll call down the guns on you."

"Everyone get out of here!" I shouted.

"I'm not getting on that fucking thing!" yelled Private Harris. "I'll take my chances with the rebels! If we get on that thing we're dead for sure!" Sergeant Michael Harris was a third-generation military man. His father and grandfather had been aviators in the C.G.. and both of them had been killed before reaching the age of thirty-five. He was an exemplary leader and an excellent NCO. But whenever he came near anything that flies, he lost control. He had to be sedated on his shuttle flights to and from orbit so that he wouldn't hurt anyone.

He was staring up at the incoming hopper, shocked. "We're all gonna die if we get on that thing! Tell me we're not getting on that fucking hopper!"

"I'm dying, Sergeant. You'll have to take command from here on out."

Mallen had gone purple. "Goddamn it, sir, you're not dying! Sergeant, look, he's not even hit!"

Earl looked at Mallen smugly. "I do believe the Lieutenant passed command to me, Corporal."

Mallen panicked, ran over to the Lieutenant, grabbed him by the collar and lifted him off the ground. "Sir, you poor stupid bastard, you're not hit!"

Lieutenant Chang, ever acceptant of his fate, merely smiled.

"Mal, you'll have to do without me. I know it's hard for you, but you just have to accept it."

The bewildered medic turned to Varney.

"Varney! Tell this stupid bastard he's not hit! Do something!"

Varney was not distracted by the pleas of Mallen and continued his recitation: "The great man down, you mark his favourite flies!" *rat-tat-tat-tat-tat-tat* "The poor advanced makes friends of enemies!" *rat-tat-tat-tat rat-tat-tat*

I crawled away from my log. "We're getting our asses handed to us." Then I saw Harris on the radio.

Rick was laying motionless in the dirt.

"Dustoff, this is Mongoose Three-Two!" Harris shouted into the radio. "Situation is lost, I repeat, situation is lost! Do not come down! Do not—"

"You bastard!" I tackled Harris and slammed my fist into his jaw. "You fucking bastard!"

Harris was down for the count.

Mallen scambled for the dropped radio. "Dustoff, this is Mongoose, ignore previous!" he shouted into the radio. "Situation not lost!"

"Mongoose, what the fuck is wrong with you? Do not play games with me! Make up your goddamn mind or I'll call the guns in on your limey ass! They'll be evacing you out of here in buckets! You want us in there or not?!"

"Roger, Dustoff, get us out of here!"

"Say again, Mongoose, I did not hear the magic word!"

Mallen couldn't believe his ears.

"What? We don't have time for this, Dustoff!"

"Correction, Mongoose, you don't have time for this. We have all the time in the world! Now what's the magic word?"

Mallen sighed. "Pl-ease. Okay? Fucking please! Please get us the goddamn hell out of here!"

"That's more like it, Mongoose! Prepare for evac!"

I was sure that I could hear laughing from the crew of the hopper over the radio, but I valued my life far more than I valued my dignity, so I let the matter go. *For now, flyboys. Only for now..*

Three hoppers came swooping in over the trees.

"Yes!" I shouted as their heavy weapons plummeled the rebel positions. "About fucking time!"

"Let's scram!" Mikael shouted.

Mallen lead the battered squads out of the bomb crater where we had been hiding.

"What's wrong with him?" the pilot asked as we entered the lead hopper, our lieutenant on a stretcher and seemingly without a scratch on him.

"He thinks he's dying!" the medic answered.

The pilot and Mallen looked at each other for a few seconds until it sank in to the pilot that he had better not ask.

The hoppers lifted, with Varney still firing his *M-90* from an open bay door.

I shook my head at the sight, still baffled by this monstrosity of a man, reciting verse after verse of Shakespeare while squeezing off salvos accurately from his machine gun, almost single-handedly decimating the enemy forces.

Lieutenant Chang once again smiled and spoke softly: "I'm glad I could die for my world."

Chapter Eleven

"The bulk of the planet is under our control."

"For now."

"The rebels broke easily enough." Collins kept his voice steady even as he glared at us. "But there are still gangs wandering around and general lawlessness in the streets. The local infrastructure has all but collapsed. That means the economy is in chaos. The restored government refuses to tolerate the situation.

"We'll need to send out patrols. You will be augmenting the local police forces. Standard rosters in full battle armour to start with."

We eyed each other.

"Rules of engagement, Sir?"

"Restraint is the order of the day." Collins paused a moment. "That being said, if you are fired upon you are authourized to return fire. Within reason!" he hastily added. "Try to wound, not kill. No collateral damage."

"There goes all the fun," Brad commented just loud enough for me to hear.

I nodded. "Yep."

Patrolling the streets wasn't so bad. We wore combat armour at the start, with assault weapons in hand, but after a couple of weeks we were usually patrolling in standard fatigues.

The bulk of the populace seemed to welcome our presence.

I was assigned to a foot patrol with Will Arsenault, from the Thirty-Fifth. He was exceedingly hot. Will was about six foot one and two hundred pounds; I also knew that Will worked out regularly and was quite strong. I had seen him the odd time in the weight room onboard the *Vindication* and his chest strained the cotton of his tee-shirt. I had never seen him naked before—never timed hitting the showers right for that—but I had heard other guys talking and he was supposed to be nicely hung.

* * *

Will and I had been on routine foot patrol through an area of Cotswald noted for its abandoned warehouses. It had become a haven for all sorts of unsavory characters...dealers, the homeless, the addicted, etc.... It was our job to sweep the area and make sure that anyone found squatting in the old buildings was removed to a shelter or somewhere else in order to prevent fires and other property damage. We had come across a doorway that appeared to have been forced, so we radioed its location back to base, and entered the building to investigate. It sounded like there were people in the basement, but it was a large building and, without lights, it was hard to find our way around. Will suggested we split up to search out the occupants, and flashlights in hands, we split up.

I wasn't very successful in finding the stairs to the basement and it took me a good ten minutes to do so. I cautiously worked my way down and listened very carefully. The voices were louder now, but still seemed to be coming from the opposite end of the building. I began to creep toward the sounds, being careful to be totally silent.

I later found out that Will had even more trouble finding a staircase than I did.

When I did eventually find one, I started down it, but had stumbled on the first step, making a dull thud with my boot and cursing softly to myself.

That was all the warning the intruders had needed.

As I reached the bottom of the stairs and turned the corner, I was struck in the face with a large fist, while being tackled around the knees by another pair of arms. I went down in a flash. My hands were pinned behind my back and cuffed with my own handcuffs, while my legs were tied together with my belt. I rolled over and saw my attackers.

There were four black youths, all about eighteen to twenty years old, all lean and sinewy, wearing what appeared to be gang colors and clothing. They had been unarmed, but now had my gun and nightstick, and were giggling and talking rapidly amongst themselves.

"You de only cop what come in here?" the apparent leader demanded.

"I'm not a cop," I replied. "I'm a marine."

"You wearin' a uniform. You a cop."

I shook my head. *So much for logic.*

"So white-boy, why you comin' in here lookin' for trouble wit us? We be mindin' our own bizness and you be messin' 'round causin' us to have to fuck wit you."

They all appeared and smelled to be at least halfway drunk, but didn't seem to be high on drugs. I hoped that Will would soon arrive and get control of the situation. *It shouldn't be taking this long for him to get here.* As I was thinking this, Will had to be getting close.

At that moment, Will stepped around the corner with his gun in his hand. "Everybody freeze!" he cried as he came around and dropped into firing position. He saw that me bound on the floor, and four black dudes gathered around him. One had an exceptionally wicked looking knife next to my throat and shook his head.

"No way, asshole. You drop de gun now or dis cop bleeds!"

Will only thought a moment before surrendering his weapon. We both knew that reinforcements would arrive within a matter of minutes if we didn't report back to headquarters with our progress on this job. If we could stall them long enough, help would arrive and everything would be ok.

"Well, you liar," the leader said to me, "you say they be no mo' cops here and in walk dis one. Now what we gonna do?"

"I know! Let's have 'em fight each other!"

"Yeah, let's make 'em fight."

"Better yet. Da winner fuck de loser. Dat be so coool, one white cop fuck anotha' white cop! We can take bets on who gonna win, this little fucker on da floor or dis big fucker standin' here wid his mouth hangin' open like a idiot!"

"We're not cops!" Will protested. "We're soldiers."

"You guyz wit guns. You cops." The leader smiled. "OK, let's see how we gonna do dis. Squatz, you and Slice take off all de cloz except his drawers on dis one here, and me an' Trip'll strip off dis big one here. An' don' nobody try an' stop us 'cause Squatz gonna cut yo buddy if you do!"

Will watched in horror as Slice pulled yet another knife out of his pants and began cutting away my shirt. It was soon a mass of shreds, and my brown under-shirt followed. The leader nodded as he studied my hairy chest and muscular body. Then they removed my boots and socks and cut away my pants, leaving me tied in just my white boxer shorts. I didn't struggle at all as Squatz kept his own knife pressed next to my throat.

Once they were finished with me, they turned to Will. As he wasn't tied, they could rip open his shirt and pull it off. His tee-shirt was next and they cut it open, exposing his well developed pecs and ripped abs.

"Oh, a muscle cop! Look like my bets gonna be on dis one!" exclaimed Slice. "Let's see what de rest of him lookin' like!"

I was actually looking forward to that as well.

Slice unfastened Will's belt, button and unzipped the fly, letting the grey pants drop to his ankles. Meanwhile, Trip had been removing his boots and socks. When finished they forced Will to step out of his pants, so he was only standing in his boxers, too.

"Okay," said the Leader, "now dat everybody ready for the fight, let's let 'em go to it! I got de gun an' anybody don't play get shot in de foot. Dey still don' play, I shoots 'em somwhere else. Squatz, let dat one you got loose so he can fight. After all, dis gonna be fair!" He started laughing at that.

I found my gag being removed, and the cuffs and belt taken off. I was allowed to stand, and turned to face Will. I knew I was no match for Will in a fight. For one thing, Will was about six foot one and two hundred pounds; I also knew that Will worked out regularly and was quite strong. I briefly began to ponder the possibilities of the two of us taking on the four black guys.

Will was also looking at the possibilities. Finally, he decided to go along with the fight. He knew they were out-manned, out-gunned, out-armed, and nearly naked! Help should be arriving soon, and if he could make the fight last long enough, they should soon have all the help they would need.

"Let's see what they packin' here," said the Leader. He approached me first and reached through my fly and groped me. I flinched at the touch of another man's hand on my cock and balls as the Leader tugged and pried at them. "I knows twelve year olds what hang better than dis cop!" he sneered. "Look to me like these white boys shouldn' have no kids if dis all dey got to fuck wit'!"

"Jealous cause I've got more than you?" I asked. I knew I was above average in size.

Slice grimaced. "Let's see what dis other fucker got!" as he approached Will. He reached into his boxers and found what he was looking for. He whistled. "Now dis be more like it! I knows my bets gonna be on this fucker. His dick be ok! Jus' so long as he don' let dat other fucker get his balls, he gonna win!"

Will, too, looked embarrassed at being groped by this man, but also a little pleased at the compliment.

"It must be real nice to have a dick and set of balls like yours," said the Leader. "I be havin' no problems wid de ladies if'n I did!

"Ok you fucks, now you fight. Winner fuck de loser in de ass. An' to help you along, have some a dis!" He grabbed a can of motor oil that had been discarded some time ago in the basement and poured half of it down Will's chest, pulling his boxers out so the oil ran down through his crotch, coating his dick and balls with the thick, slick fluid. The remainder he poured down my chest, repeating the procedure. He then massaged each of our crotches, making sure our boxers were soaked and our cocks well-oiled. "Start now, an' remember, anybody try anything, I shoots de other man in de foot!"

Will and I eyed each other warily. He clearly didn't want this to be happening, though I would have enjoyed more privacy. Finally Will lunged at me, grabbed me, and spun me around. He was able to whisper to him while doing so. "Just put up a fight, Lou. We'll both stall and help should get here before we have to do anything serious!"

I grunted in reply and attempted an escape of Will's hold. We spun apart, and slowly began circling.

"Come on you fucks!" cried the Leader, "you best get started here or we gonna finish da job fo' you!"

Shit, I thought. *They're not going to let us stall at all*! I decided to go on the offensive and grabbed at Will, forcing him to his knees. "Easy buddy, I've got to make this look halfway good," I said as I struggled to contain Will's swinging arms. He was attempting to fight back, and Will had a good height/weight advantage, and most of his efforts were devoted to escape only.

Just then a shot rang out!

"I said hurry the fuck up! We ain't got all night to watch you white boys dance! If somebody don't get fucked real fast, they gonna find a bullet up dey ass!"

Will got the message, and so did I. Both of us attacked, chests pressed together, crotches mashed against each others' thighs as their arms struggled for domination. Will's advantages soon overcame my efforts as I was forced back onto the floor. Will quickly turned me over and jerked my boxers down, exposing my ass to the assembled group.

"No!" I cried out, trying to make things look good, but Will pulled my shorts completely off, leaving me naked. He then pinned my arms with his own and settled over his body, crotch to ass, chest to back. He whispered "I hope help gets here fast...I don't know how much longer I can stall."

I sighed in anguish, not knowing what to expect next.
"So come on fucker, get on with it!"
"I can't, I can't get hard!" Will replied.
"Well your buddy best make it hard, less'n I hafta shoot it."
I nodded with feigned reluctance. "Okay, I'll suck it!"
Will was surprised at the reply, but thought that he understood what I was doing. Will pulled out his dick and shoved it at my face. I tentatively licked at it, nearly retching at the taste of the motor oil that was all over it. Still, I managed to get the head into my mouth and began to suck half-heartedly. Will was surprised at his cock's response to my mouth. He had never felt queer in his life, but his dick was getting stiff almost instantly! "This won't help at all!" he hissed to me. He was obviously trying to think of other things, but his dick easily won the contest and was soon fully hard and beginning to drool pre-cum. My eyes had widened as the dick in his mouth grew larger and larger. His plan had failed...time to make the best of it.

The Leader saw what had happened and said "Look hard enough to me now. So fuck him!"

Will withdrew from my mouth. "I'll do it, but I need to do it real slow. He's never had a dick up his ass and I don't want to hurt him."

Shows what you know, I thought.

"Okay," sneered the Leader. He watched as Will turned me onto my stomach again and moved back into position over my ass. He gently nudged his throbbing dick against my sphincter and pushed slightly. I felt a brief moment of terror race through my body at the thought of Will's big dick shoving into my asshole, but tried to relax.

"Easy buddy, I'll go real slow, just relax and let it happen."

At that moment, the Leader came up and shoved Will's ass with all his strength!

Will's dick which had been perfectly positioned rammed completely into my ass in one quick motion, sinking all the way in to Will's balls.

I almost blacked out.

"You fucker," Will yelled. "I'm gonna kill you for this!" and tried to back out of me, but the Leader held him firmly in place, while the others gathered around and helped hold Will's arms and legs, keeping him from struggling much.

Then, the Leaded lifted Will's hips and pulled him partway out, then shoved him in again. "If'n you don' fuck him, I'll help you do it!" He continued raising and lowering Will's hips.

I shook my head to clear it and cried out in agony with each thrust of Will's cock. *This is not how it's supposed to be!*

Everyone else was enjoying themselves immensely, watching one white soldier fuck the other. The oil was getting slicker with the heat of our bodies, and we were now well-coated with it.

Will must have been getting close to cumming and suddenly felt the Leader pull him completely from me. His dick popped out with a slight sucking sound and Rickbed in the air, wildly looking for the warm hole it had been so rudely removed from. Slice and Squatz both tied my arms together, as the Leader and Trip pulled Will away. The other two then tied my legs, immobilizing me. They then removed their own clothes, revealing lean, sinewy bodies with hard dicks waving in front of them. Neither was over seven inches, but both were fairly thick.

Squatz leered. "Now it's my turn," and crawled onto me. He wiped some of the oil onto his dick, and then shoved it in. I yelled again, but I was helpless to defend myself and could only lay there and hope it would end soon.

Meanwhile, the other three were turning their attentions to Will.

"Yeah, dis dick gonna have a good time yet! Look at how it like to be touched!" the Leader said as he played with Will's hard cock. Slice reached down and grabbed Will's balls, squeezing them tightly. Will moaned in pain, and received a slap across the face for his trouble. "Shut up!" They then ripped off his boxers and forced him to the floor on his back. Trip sat across Will's chest, facing him, slapping his dick back and forth across Will's face. Meanwhile Slice sat directly behind Trip, facing Will's dick. He grabbed it with both hands and began stroking it. The Leader pried Will's legs apart and held them up in "V", exposing his ass and balls. The Leader wasted no time. He greased his dick, positioned it over the hole, and shoved against the tight resistance.

He wiped more oil through Will's crack and tried a third time. This time, his dick-head got all the way in before Will clamped back down. Now he was stuck. He couldn't back out because Will's sphincter had him tightly held just below the crown of his cock, and he couldn't go further in because his shaft thickened rapidly. He was being forced to fuck with just his dick-head! The sensation was weird. "Pull his tits!" he yelled, while grabbing the nuts that were laying in front of him. As he squeezed the balls, Trip pulled and twisted Will's nipples. His sphincter gave up, relaxed, and the Leader shoved all the way in.

He began to fuck slowly, hitting Will's prostate with each thrust. He looked quite thrilled with the control and domination he had over the white cop. He transferred Will's legs to Slice and wrapped his black fingers around Will's rigid pink shaft, rubbing his fingers over Wills red and swollen glans. His other hand continued to squeeze the large balls, as his dick slowly slid in and out.

Will was going wild with frustration and sensation. He opened his mouth to yell and Trip shoved his dick in. "You bite it, you die!" Will allowed his mouth to be fucked, feeling Trip's dick slide into his throat. He tried not to gag, but couldn't help it. Trip didn't care and kept up the assault. Slice held Will's legs as far apart as possible, watching the black fingers of his leader stroking up and down the glistening white dick. It was amazing how fragile a white cock looked. All veins and red and helpless!

I was able to notice that Will's balls barely fit into the Leader's hand, but they too were all defenceless looking. Will was totally unable to move. Trip began working his tits again while still fucking his face. His dick was leaking like mad now and his balls were struggling to settle in next to the base of his cock so they could unload, but the Leader kept them pulled away. His prostate was going wild with the continued pounding it was receiving, and his whole body began to vibrate with tension.

Suddenly, Trip shuddered and he shot his load down Will's throat. Meanwhile, the Leader began cumming, slamming as hard as he could into Will's virgin ass as he shot his load into Will's guts. As he shot, his grip on Will's dick increased, as did his stroking tempo. His hand clamped decisively around the base of Will's balls, squeezing the helpless nuts tight into their sack.

Slice released my legs and pressed firmly against mys navel and the bone right at the base of my dick. I went over the edge. I heard myself scream as the first volley exploded from my cock and hit Squatz square in the mouth. The second shot hit him in the chest, the third hit Slice in the chest, and the rest left descending strings of sticky cum trailing down the Squatz's chest.

It was then that we heard other sounds in the room as our reinforcements finally arrived. Will lifted his head and glanced around and saw several other soldiers charging into the room, each with horrified looks of shock and dismay written plainly on their faces. The humiliation and embarrassment were too much for him, coming right on the heels of his tremendous orgasm, and his mind shut down, blocking the entire night's events from his waking memory.

Chapter Twelve

"Some adventure you had, Lou."

I nodded and sipped my beer. The bar was crowded with off-duty marines and base personnel. "An foreseen hazard," I agreed. "I hadn't expected to be raped while on duty." Although I'd had more than a few hot jack-off sessions with the memories since then.

Brad shook his head. "I can't imagine what that must have been like for you."

"It wasn't that bad."

"Will is still on psych leave."

"I must be made of harder stuff than him."

Brad smiled. "Nah, you just like that kind of thing."

I shrugged and offered him a cocky grin. "Maybe."

"So what was the worst part of it all?"

"I'm not sure. The most embarrassing part had to be returning to base in just my boots." That was the only part of my uniform still intact. *Three hundred credits to buy a new uniform...shit.*

"Good thing you got no shame, Lou."

"Yeah." I leaned back in the chair. "Good thing." I scratched my crotch then reached for my beer.

I staggered into the barracks and threw myself onto the bunk. I thought back to my early training...

I choked the veiny shaft and swabbed my tongue over the spongy cockhead.

"Keep licking it. Put it in your mouth and suck it."

I did what the sergeant asked. It tasted icky—the rubber—and I hated it. But I have to admit I liked sucking his big dick. He got into a sixty-nine position and put a rubber on my cock. When he put his hot, wet mouth on my cock, I thought I'd shoot for sure; my cock just quivered. Together we sucked each other and I wasn't very good at it, maybe because his cock was so big, but he expertly swallowed me. I gagged when I tried to do the same to him.

He let go of my dick and stroked it with his hand. "Blow me, Lou. Make me cum, soldier boy."

I let go of his sheathed dick and jacked it. It was so big I don't know how the rubber kept from breaking, being stretched over that fat fucker. "Suck me off, Sarge."

Together we both went back to work on each other's cock. I stopped gagging on the rubber. He deep-throated my big dick all the way down to the balls and even managed to get part of them into his mouth. I was hotter than hell; I couldn't hold back.

I grabbed his nuts and squeezed them, with his cock entrenched in my throat.

That's when all hell broke loose. His cock fell out of my mouth and it literally

exploded, creaming that rubber tip, filling it with white jizz. Seeing that got me right off. He kept my cock in his throat and I unloaded my nuts, flooding that rubber with gobs and gobs of jism. Jason snapped the rubber off his fat prick and slung the cum across my hairy chest. I did the same to him.

"I had no idea it could feel so good, getting it on with another man," I said as we lay there exhausted and sweaty.

"That's just the beginning," he grinned back at me.

"You do it with other soldiers?"

"Not much. I ain't no slut. I waited a long time for you, to give it to you,

and now you're going to get it." Jason rolled me over onto my belly and then spread eagled me before I knew what happened.

"You can't rape me."

"No one's raping you. Say the word and I'll stop."

"No, don't stop. I'm just scared. Your dick's so big."

"Big ones hurt less, believe me. Little dingys are like knives."

"I don't care if it hurts. I gotta have it. Fuck me, Sarge." I couldn't believe my ears. I was begging to be fucked, begging to be buggered by my sergeant. I must be losing my mind. Jason was an expert butt-fucker, no doubt about it. He spit on my tiny hole and worked it with his fingers. He got some grease out of that table drawer and more rubbers. Before long his cock was bone-hard and covered with another rubber.

My virgin hole was greased up and ready for assault. His cock didn't hurt as much as I thought it would, entering me. The flared cockhead stretched my hole. He waited before he lunged his shaft deeper. "Aw fuck, you're killing me," I screamed.

He put his arm under my face and told me to bite it. I bit his hairy arm and

the pain subsided in my asshole. It was burning, ready to be pumped and

quenched. The pain of penetration subsided and I was delirious with the sergeant's cock crammed in my ass.

"Fuck me, Jason. Let me have it. I want it. I can take it. Fuck the shit out

of me."

The sarge met the challenge. He pistoned my hole and his cock got bigger and even harder, if that was possible. Despite the rubber, I could feel the heat

and knew he'd fill the rubber with his load soon.

"Do it. Shoot it up my ass. Oh, Sarge. Ohhh!" My guts were creamed with his juice. I could feel it despite the rubber.

Moaning, he slowly pulled out. Looking over my shoulder, I watched him tug off the rubber and drip his wad all over my butt cheeks and baste them with the goo, making them sticky.

Jason had fucked me into a big hard-on. When I turned over I think he was a tad intimidated by its size and strength. "Your turn, Sarge."

"Christ. I don't go for that shit." He grinned and I knew that he was egging me on. No way was he going to make a pussy boy out of me. I'd show him my mettle. Fueled by lust and hot for the sergeant, I got him on his belly. I sheathed my cock and greased his hole. Then I stuffed it.

"Oh yeah, do it, soldier-boy!" Jason cried out. "Fuck this GI butt. Give me all you got."

Jason got the roughest fucking I'd ever given anybody. I rammed him

relentlessly and he took it all, every inch of my randy private's prick. "Feel it? Feel me shooting up your ass, Sarge?"

My balls banged against his hairy butt and I gushed with such an onslaught that I was scared the rubber would burst. It didn't.

When I finally plopped out of his well-fucked hole, I was a little afraid of him because I'd come on so strong and balled him so hard.

Jason smiled at me. "You're everything I hoped you'd be and more, Lou."

This time I grabbed him and held him and kissed him, letting him know that this was no one-way romance, no one-night stand.

And it hadn't been. For nearly half a year, the sergeant's pad had been our private love nest. He taught me a lot about cooking and making love, and I think he learned a bit from me too. What I had lacked in experience I more than made up for in enthusiasm and experimenting. I had been crushed when he got orders to go spaceward to the frontier.

I got over him eventually.

Just like I got over Brad and Jeff and Rick.

* * *

Patrols were stepped up. After the incident in the industrial district, the military government had begun a more aggressive patrolling routine. We were sent out in half-squads and in full battle armour.

It was a little embarrassing actually.

Still, we had little choice. Securing the planet was a top priority for us.

The civilians seemed all right with our presence. It was just a few scattered malcontents who protested us.

Mikael and I were on patrol.

The spaceport was back to normal operations and we were manning one of the security checkpoints at the southwest gates.

"Stuck in a war on Elysia while the woman of my dreams is in danger."

I looked over at Mikael. "Are you still going on about that reporter?"

"You're fucking right that I am." He shook his head. "She's there; I'm here. It's not fucking fair."

"Life isn't fair." I held up my hand as a car approached the gate. It slowed to a stop with a squeal of brakes. "Let's see your travel permit."

"This is ridiculous." The man glared at me. "I've got business with StarAdmin."

"The Administration can confirm your appointment?"

Mikael was grinning behind his now-closed visor.

"Of course they can."

"Let me see your permit." I kept my voice neutral.

The civilian was sweating.

"I have business."

"It can wait."

The car drove through the checkpoint.

"You enjoyed that."

"Yep." I raised my visor and looked squarely at Mikael. "So did you."

"Yeah." He smiled. "You had him shaking." He chuckled. "I never thought you had such a mean streak."

"That wasn't mean of me. I was just playing with him."

"Did I ever tell you about Darlene?"

"No." I sighed softly, recognizing the look in his eyes. He was going to go off on some story about one of his conquests.

"Well, back when I was in high school, I was getting dressed to meet up with this chick named Darlene for our study date. Course, I was wishing that the only thing I had to study was Darlene. It was my birthday and it was a shame that I had to ruin it studying."

"You studied?"

He didn't respond. "I decided on a pair of smiley face boxers, black jeans, and a red tank top—hoping that we could ditch the clothes and our books. I put on my sandals, grabbed my backpack, and headed across campus.

"When I got to Darlene's room, there was a note on the door that she was at the "beach"—that was an area the girls had set up behind the dorm to sunbathe—and I should join her there. I was kinda ticked cause I would have worn some shorts instead, but seeing Darlene in a bikini was enough to calm my anger. Cheryl stuck her head out of her room and said that she wanted to make sure I found the note. I said that I had and headed down stairs to join Darlene.

"I spotted her not too far away from the door. She was looking for me and waved me on over. She had on a new bikini that I had not seen before, a hot pink number that should give her a great tan because it didn't cover very much. With her blond hair, that bikini, and her glistening skin from the suntan lotion, I was suddenly glad that I had on the jeans after all so I wouldn't embarrass myself in front of the other girls on the beach. She looked at me and said 'Do you really want to study on your birthday? The weather is supposed to get cooler next week so I wanted to get in some last minute tanning to take me through the fall and winter.'

"I said, in my most sarcastic tone, that I really did, but for her sake I would go with the flow. As I took off my shirt, I said that I was sorry that I didn't come better dressed. She shut me up by telling me that we could always go inside and study. I sat down next to her without another word.

"Then she asked how my birthday was going and I told her that so far it was just another day, but it might be looking up.

"She laughed. 'I want to do my part to make this a special day for you.'

"'Oh, what do have in mind?' I could already feel some stirrings in my crotch and reconciled myself to some wet underwear.

"She told me to roll over onto my stomach and she squeezed a huge plop of suntan lotion that felt incredible. My stirrings were starting to solidify. She sat on my rear and rubbed the lotion all over my back, neck and arms. She was being playful and rubbed it up in my hair, and even played with the band of my boxers. I was quite lost in the moment of building pleasure when she told me to turn over. She was giving me the same treatment on my front after kissing both my pecks and our tongues becoming one when I told her that I was approaching the point of no return.

"She smiled at me and said that it was the whole point. I released like never before and the only regret was that I was wearing black jeans that I knew the cum stain would show on them. I was so happy at that moment that I missed part two shaping up.

"Darlene asked me if I was happy. What a question to ask! I was greased up top and gooey below and I have to admit that I thought that was the dumbest question I had ever been asked. All I could say was 'Fucking yeah'.

"'Good, here is the rest.' And then I heard strains of lovely feminine voices start singing "Happy Birthday." Darlene stayed where she was as this group of girls came out of the stairway carrying a birthday cake and some other stuff. They finished the song and I leaned over and blew out the single candle on top. Darlene reach over and ran her finger through the icing and then ran it down the centre of my chest. I couldn't believe I was getting hard again after such a wonderful release. As I was just wondering what exactly was getting ready to come down, the girls holding the cake upended it from the middle of my chest to the top of my head.

"With a cheer and a good bit of laughter, I was suddenly getting rubbed down with my own cake. Darlene grabbed the bag and I suddenly got a chill as melted ice cream was poured and rubbed down my back. Lastly, I was turned into a turtle sundae as caramel and chocolate syrup was being poured over my head, down my pants legs, and most importantly, down my jeans and boxers. When the bottles were empty Darlene started her hand motion again and I came again.

"I fell back with the dumbest grin possible and could barely get the thanks out to the girls."

I shook my head in disbelief. "You are amazing."

"I've been told that before. Not usually by men though." Mikael leered at me. "The walk back across campus, under normal circumstances, would have been pretty humiliating; however, I wore it as a badge of honour and I certainly wasn't worried about any cum stains showing through the cake, ice cream, and the syrup."

"And that was it?'

"Well, when the guys in the dorm saw me, they all went ape shit. When they heard the story, everyone went pea green with envy, and I showered for a long time in peace."

"Fuck." I just shook me head.

"True story," Mikael swore.

Chapter Thirteen

I had stayed late at the gym to do some extra working out. There were very few, if any, other soldiers using the building that night, so I had most of the equipment to myself.

I was just leaving the weight room when it happened.

First the lights dimmed. I dismissed it as a just a malfunction. The emergency generators would kick in after a few moments.

Them I was jumped from behind by two, perhaps three individuals.

I struggled and thrashed about, but I was held fast and manhandled into another room and dragged over to the bench press portion of the Universal gym. I cried out several times as my wrists were tied securely to the push bar. My legs were held down, and my ankles bound to the each side of the bench.

I could barely move, and now stopped my struggling momentarily, and looked confusedly at the two males standing in front of me. They were wearing masks.

"What the fuck are—" Then a sweaty sock was stuffed into my mouth one of them moved toward me and lifted my t-shirt over my head, cutting off my vision.

I froze in shock at that.

His hands then moved down and pulled down my cotton shorts and boxers so they were at my knees. I cried out as they both knelt on either side of me, and began to probe my prone form with their hands.

I became frantic as I felt one hand trace it's way down my body, coming to rest on my soft cock. It began to squeeze and pull gently at me, causing me to buck and thrash in a vain attempt to free myself. I tried to plead with them to stop this assault, but they said nothing.

I cried out, but my muffled shrieks were ignored.

I felt their tongues and mouths begin to lick and suck at my nipples. They were extraordinarily sensitive, and I squirmed and writhed at the feel of it. The one hand continued to manipulate my penis, and despite my adamant protests, it began to swell.

Several minutes of licking and sucking yielded an almost fully erect cock, and when they noticed this, their attention immediately became focused on it. They began to alternate sucking and licking my swollen penis. One would take him in my mouth for several seconds, then retreat so the other would have a turn. I was struggling desperately to ward off the sensation, but it was to no avail. I could slowly feel it welling up inside him, and there was nothing I could do to stop it.

My protests had been reduced to cries of meaningless gibberish as they continued at an ever increasing and rapid pace. My erection began to throb violently, and my last futile attempt to block out the sensation failed. It was starting, and I could do nothing to stop it.

I let out a loud groan, and they immediately pulled their mouths away, replacing it with one of their hands. The hand gripped my cock firmly, and began to roughly tug and pull on it. I let out a guttural moan, and I squirmed crazily as I felt it well up inside.

I let out an explosive gasp, and my legs and arms strained at their bonds. My hips thrust upward, and the first spurt of cum erupted from my erection, coating the head with the sticky white substance. My own cum was now being used as lubricant as the hand smeared it over the head and continued. Another spurt and frantic groan from him, then a third and fourth.

"Look at him shoot."

"Nice, dude, very nice."

I could hear them murmurs of approval came from the two as they continued pulling at him, coating the lower part of my stomach with my hot man-juice.

I collapsed helplessly back onto the bench, my breathing shallow and rapid. Aftershocks from the intense orgasm coursed through me. I had no idea what my assailants were up too. Not until after I felt a great weight press down on my chest, and realized that one of them was now laying on top of me. Naked.

His hips began to thrust against my stomach, and it took only half a minute before another eruption of cum began to spurt onto my stomach and chest, though this time it was not my own. The one on top of me continued to thrust until the contents had emptied over me. I felt weak and exhausted by this experience, and wanted to crawl away and hide somewhere, but they were not done yet.

They seized my legs, and after untying them from the bench. Brought them upward, fastening them to the press bar. I had a bad feeling of what was about to happen, but could do little to stop it. They began to scoop up the sticky white substance with their fingers, and I felt them begin to smear it on my anus. I shrieked, now desperately pleading in my muffled voice for them to stop.

They ignored me.

A tentative finger began to probe my ass, and I grunted as I felt it.

A moment later, the feeling was five times more intense. I felt a stiff erection push at my butt, then slide inside and begin to thrust. My loud grunts and groans appeared to have no effect, save for spurring them on. The thrusting became faster, and I began crying out, feeling like I was being split in two. Grunts were coming from elsewhere, though, and a scant few seconds later I felt the erection bury itself deeply inside me. I could actually feel the cum spurting out inside me. Several more quick thrusts emptied the contents of the erection inside me.

My tee-shirt was pulled down and I blinked at the light.

"Did you like it?"

I stared at my attacker.

"I thought you would enjoy that." Jeff was smiling. With his blond-hair, blue-eyes, square-jaw, and slender build, he was still the cutest thing I had ever seen in my days in the military.

"You?" I spluttered as the sock was removed my mouth.

"I've heard a lot of stories about you."

"I haven't heard anything about you." I lifted my head and looked around, but Jeff's friend was gone. "It's been forever."

"I wanted to make my return memorable."

"When did you get in?"

"A few hours ago." Jeff brushed his fingers along my chest and watched me squirm. "I don't report back to duty until tomorrow. How about we go back to your quarters and get...reacquainted?"

"Sounds like a plan to me."

Also by Frank Sol

Novels Of The Sensual City
A Family Affair
Delivering The Goods
Divine Punishment
Good Neighbours
Just Between Friends
Landscaping, Manscaping
Titan's Cradle - A Novel of the Sensual Suns
Terran Cummando - A Novel Of The Sensual Suns

Novels On The Prairies
Bareback Range
Return To Bareback Range
Fenced In

www.ingramcontent.com/pod-product-compliance
Lightning Source LLC
Chambersburg PA
CBHW052100150726
48002CB00002B/964